TO: anne with best wishes
and thanks from Joe
3rd oct. 2009

LOST IN IRELAND

A

Tale of World War II

A Novel

by

Joe O'Loughlin

Lost in Ireland A Tale of World War II
© 2007 Joe O' Loughlin
ISBN 978-0-9546605-2-9

Design & Layout:
Diamond SignPrinting Ltd. (James McGrath)

Illustrations:
Jane O' Loughlin

Introduction

THE PHANTOM AIR PLANE

The Final Flight of a JUNKERS 88a.

In the Castle Caldwell district of Belleek, Co. Fermanagh, Northern Ireland, local folklore tells a story of a German aircraft that reputedly crashed in the Croagh More, which is a marshy moorland in the North West of County Fermanagh. This place of several hundred acres in size is very close to the border with the Free State of Ireland at County Donegal.

The story goes: - *That the four - man crew escaped either by parachute or from the aero-plane when it crash - landed. It is said to have sunk in the soft moorland and disappeared without trace. The four Germans made their way across the border into Eire, as it was then known. There they called to the house of a local farmer.*

Many years later the farmer produced a number of German mark notes claiming that the Germans had given them to him as a reward for his help. However, the local bank declared these to be post-World War 1 notes and therefore useless. For years such notes were sold in novelty shops all over the country. The Irish Gardai {police} has no record of any German airmen being taken into custody in Donegal during World War 11. Nor do the comprehensive records held in the Irish Military Archives in Cathal Brugha Barracks in Dublin have any information on such an incident. Similarly the German Prisoner of War camp in the Curragh, Co. Kildare had no record of such a crew.

I have spoken personally to people who live in the area. Some are convinced that a plane did crash; others are very skeptical about the matter; quite a few sensible and dependable people are adamant that it never happened. None of those who say they witnessed the crash can give a time, a day, a date, a week, a month or even a year for the incident. No piece of wreckage has ever been produced to support the theory. Over the years, the reputed site has been investigated by the police and air force experts. Aviation historians equipped with metal detectors and long probes have failed to find any trace of anything in the moorland apart from the smell of oil or fuel on the probes, which can be linked to an entirely different wartime episode.

When Sunderland NJ 175 from nearby Castle Archdale crashed in the vicinity on 12th August 1944, it had circled the area as it jettisoned fuel and depth charges. There is a strong possibility that a quantity of fuel and one of the depth charges dropped at the reputed crash site. This could convince people in all sincerity that a plane did crash here and account for the smell of fuel. In 1946 a small single engine private plane did crash in the Ballagee mountain; about half a mile west as the crow flies from the Curragh More, but the two fishermen aboard escaped without injury.

Until there is evidence found to the contrary, I shall have my doubts about any such incident concerning a German WWII plane ever having had happened. I have consulted with several noted aviation historians on both sides of the border and they have no knowledge of any such crash having taken place. Records show that during several wartime air raids on Belfast, not one German plane was shot down. Also, in the course of the whole war; only one German aero-plane was lost north of a line from Dundalk to Galway. This was in July 1940 a German Focke-Wulf 200 Condor was on a mine laying exercise in Belfast Lough. Due to engine failure it crashed into the sea about 15 miles north east of Belfast. Two of the crew died and three including the pilot Hauptman Volkmar Zenker escaped from the plane. The three were captured and became prisoners of war.

In spite of all that I am sure that there is the material for a fictional novel based on such a story for Irish folklore and the following is my idea of what might have happened.

Preface

Joe O'Loughlin's story is centered on the topic of kindness to strangers. This is a subject he handles with ease because Joe's own kindness to strangers is part and parcel of his nature. Joe regularly goes out of his way to give a welcome and information to anyone seeking their roots in Belleek, Co. Fermanagh. His account of human compassion and personal courage in Lost in Ireland reflects Joe's dedication to ordinary people and his great love of the places around his home. He has thoroughly researched the historical and technical aspects of the book, creating a fictional story of wartime adventure set around Lough Erne. The book reflects Joe's extensive knowledge of wartime aero-plane crash sites in Fermanagh, His kindness in sharing his research with many World War 11 air force veterans and their families is well known locally. I like to think that the words of J.M. Barrie apply to Joe: "Those who bring sunshine into the lives of others; cannot keep it from themselves."

Jean Gorman - September 2006

Chapter 1

The making of a pilot in the German Lufftwaffe

Ernst Schmitt was born in 1918, the son of Dieter and Elsa Schmitt. His father had been a member of an engineering unit in the German army during the 1914 – 1918 world war. Wounded at the Battle of Cambrai in 1917, Dieter was evacuated from the front and returned to his native town of Pulheim which is situated about 30 kilometers north west of the city of Köln. His mechanical engineering experience enabled him to set up a small workshop where he manufactured components for motorcars and motorcycles. His services were often called upon to repair damaged farm machinery. The years after the war were extremely difficult. New parts could not be obtained; Dieter used his ingenuity to make many of the required items.

He found some very useful items of equipment in surplus army stores where they could be bought at reasonable prices. His workshop contained many precision tools such as lathes, drills, hydraulic presses and welding gear. From an early age his son Ernst showed a keen interest in engineering and he had the natural ability to operate machinery. The 1920's were very difficult years with money being hard to earn. There was a depression not only in Germany, but in many of the leading countries in the world. When Adolf Hitler came into power in 1933 there developed a great change in Germany. Employment improved, as did the manufacturing industry. As a result of his experience in the Great War, Dieter had developed a tendency to be pacifist in nature. He had seen enough of the horrors and suffering of war. As he observed how the Nazis took control of the country and how they started to persecute members of the Jewish race and other people he decided to keep a low profile and not get involved with the party. As his son Ernst grew up and during his formative years his father carefully advised him on the dangers of warfare and to avoid situations whereby he would be unduly influenced by the Youth organizations that were springing up in Germany.

When the time came for Ernst to continue his education at a higher level, in consultation with his parents it was decided that he should get a place in the Technical College in the nearby city of Köln rather than enroll in a University. The Technical College had a first class engineering department where one of the leading lecturers was a good friend of Dieter's. It was a non-residential institution and being in easy traveling distance from Pulheim it was no problem for the 16 year old Ernst to attend the college and still live in his family home. The danger of attending a University was that he would have to reside there and so could come under undue influence from the many student groups who were becoming increasingly involved in politics.

Normally the young student would cycle the 10 kilometer journey to the college except in the winter months or during unusually bad weather when he would take the bus. He settled in well to the course and it soon became obvious to his lecturer that he had an inventive mind and a natural flair for working with metals of any kind. At home in the evenings and at the weekends he would discuss with his father the different projects that he was working on. Ernst was able to recommend to his father some improvements that could be made in the family business and advise on new and more modern equipment. In the college there were a number of recreational clubs that catered for a large selection of interests. Ever since he had been given a present of a camera for his 12th birthday Ernst had become a keen photographer, therefore he applied for and was accepted as a member of the College camera club. The club members naturally were involved in many outdoor activities including swimming, something that the young engineering student was also keen on.

At home Ernst had many discussions with his parents about his studies, his future and the developing political situation in Germany. From his experience over the years Dieter could foresee the trend that things were taking. He advised his son against becoming a member of any of the extreme youth groups that were now increasingly popular. He warned him that in any of the work places and clubs there were always members who reported anything of interest to the authorities. As the family lived in a small community they were not under the same pressure as would have been the case in a large city. Nevertheless when the two men had anything of importance to discuss they would always go for a walk in the nearby park rather than talk in the workshop.

As Ernst was reaching the end of his course in the Technical College it was understood that after graduation he would by law have to join one or other of the military services. About this time Dieter had gained a contract manufacturing components for aircraft. The finished products had to be delivered to an airfield south east of the city of Köln. When Ernst learned how to drive he delivered the parts in the factory van. This led to him having a great interest in aero-planes and he got to know many of the pilots and air crew members. Following several discussions with his father it was decided that when his time came to join the military he should apply for a place in the Luftwaffe.

At the college in the spring weather Ernst would often go to the Pulheim market place which was near the famous Dom, as the Cathedral was known. Here he could sit at one of the open air tables and enjoy his mid-day meal. On one nice day when all the tables were occupied, he was approached by a very pleasant looking young lady who asked if the unoccupied seat was free. She was tall, her dark hair cut stylishly and pleasingly short and she wore a polo - necked jumper and a matching skirt. Ernst confirmed that the seat was free and invited her to have it. Soon they got talking and it transpired that she was also a student at the college where she was studying languages. She introduced herself saying, “My name is Gabriela Helling and I live with my mother, Susanna in Friedrich Street here in the city.” Ernst gave her his name and where he lived and told of the course he was doing at the college. Gabriela said, “I study several languages including Spanish, French, Italian and English”. The young couple found that they had many common interests and they found each other’s company pleasing. Soon it was time to return to their lectures. As they parted they arranged to meet again.

The young couple became good friends and shared many common interests. They learned about each other’s families and their backgrounds. Gabriela told that her mother worked as a secretary in a legal firm. Her father, Albrecht had been of the Jewish faith, but sadly he had been killed in an accident in 1932 when Gabriela was only twelve years of age. Naturally she missed him very much. She herself had gone on several educational trips to foreign lands to gain experience in different languages. She had an ambition to visit Canada for her mother’s sister lived in the city of Toronto. Aunt Margret had imigrated to Canada in the early 1920’s. There she met and married a young Irish man named Peter O’Reilly. They had two children, Eva and Michael who were just a few years younger than Gabriela. Margret was due to come on holiday to her native Germany early in 1938. Gabriela hoped that after her graduation she would go for a holiday with her Aunt to Canada. There she would get valuable experience in the use of the English language. Of course the trip would have to be approved of by the German authorities. This should not be a problem as they were anxious to have young people proficient in foreign languages.

Chapter 2

The Friendship Develops

Ernst and Gabriela continued to work at their studies for it was important to get a good mark in examinations. Gabriela had found part time work in a city bookshop, it was necessary that she should earn and save money to pay expenses when traveling abroad. By helping in his fathers engineering works Ernst was able to get a small wage. As they got to know each other better the young couple visited each other's homes. Susanna, the mother of Gabriela found Ernst to be a very agreeable young man; in the household he made another new friend. This was Rex the family pet dog; he was a Springer Spaniel, a most affectionate animal who took to Ernst right away. At the weekends when the young people had spare time to go walking in the park, Rex would always accompany them.

On visits to the Schmitt home Gabriela soon became a great favourite with Dieter and Elsa. She loved to hear Dieter tell of his travels and experiences during the war years. She also learned much about the political situation in Germany and she got some idea of the difficulties that were developing. Dieter soon became a second father to her; all though she was young when her own father died she had been very close to him.

Ernst made excellent progress with his studies and soon became one of the leading students in the engineering class. Much of his knowledge could be put to good use in the aircraft industry which was rapidly developing. With his membership of the camera club he increased his skills in photography. He progressed from his first camera to one of the latest Zeiss-Ikon cameras. This camera manufactured in the city of Dresden was the most modern equipment that it was possible to have. When they had some free time Gabriela would accompany him on the countryside outings with the club. During these trips Gabriela would teach him how to improve his knowledge of the English language. They both felt that in the future this could be useful.

Being like his father, a pacifist, Ernst having studied all the aspects of the different military groups decided that the air force was best suited to him. There were opportunities in that force to develop skills in navigation, photography and reconnaissance. By concentrating on these subjects he could make himself invaluable in the force and not get into life taking exercises.

The young couple continued to meet regularly. They visited each others homes and the families became firm friends. Gabriela often brought Rex along and they took him with them for walks in the nearby woods. Ernst was quite fond of animals and enjoyed the company of the dog. The young people did not neglect their studies and worked hard to prepare for the examinations which would take place in the autumn of 1937. Gabriela and Ernst conversed often in English when they were alone together for he wanted to become proficient in that language. She taught him how to speak the language without much trace of a German accent. In those years many of the songs popular with young people were broadcast from England and America, therefore Gabriela would adopt the style of the songs in their speech. They also listened to the world news broadcast by English Radio Stations. Both of them had a great love for their homeland as it had been in the past, but not as it was developing under the new regime. They had to be careful when in the company of others not to express their true feelings.

Dieter and his son often discussed the political situation, from a life time of experience Dieter could foresee the trend that the country was taking. He knew there was nothing he or his family could do about it; only continue with the running of their business. Ernst became friendly with the staff at the air base when he was delivering the spare parts for the planes. The mechanics and the pilots soon took an interest in the young man who was so knowledgeable about air craft. There were occasions when they were able to take him along with them on short test flights, all unofficial of course.

Chapter 3

The College Years

Soon it was time for Gabriela to take her examinations, she had studied well and her lecturer had every confidence that she would get a high mark. Ernst and she did not have much spare time to socialize; there was so much work to be done. Ernst had both written and practical work to do. For him it was a great advantage to have the use of his father's workshop and equipment. He had also taken an extra course in photography and while this was very important he was not under any pressure, it was more for him a recreation and a means to relax.

There was regular communication between Gabriela, her mother and Aunt Margret in Canada. Her aunt's plan was to come home on a visit in the spring of 1938, bring the children with her and spend almost five weeks in Germany. All being well and if she had got permission to travel abroad, Gabriela would join her aunt on the return voyage to Canada. Susanna gave her every encouragement and support; they talked it over many times. Susanna was aware of the campaign being carried out against the Jewish people and was afraid that with her daughter's Jewish ancestry she could be in extreme danger.

Gabriela sat her examinations in early autumn and she felt that she had done well. It was near Christmas when she got her results, which were excellent. So good were her marks that she was in the top four in her class. This meant that she was held in high esteem not only by the college but also by the government authorities. For her graduation there was a nice party with her mother, a few cousins, special friends and of course Ernst along with his parents. Gabriela applied for permission to spend a year with her aunt in Canada so as to gain more experience in English and also in French; which was a second language in that country. Her college lectures were most supportive of this and with their high recommendation she got official approval to spend at least a year with her aunt.

Many letters were exchanged between Köln and Toronto and the final plans were made. Margret booked the passage on one of the great ocean liners. It was due to leave Halifax on 1st March 1938 on the Trans-Atlantic voyage. With Margret would come the children, Eva and Michael. Her Irish born husband, Peter O'Reilly was coming part way. The liner was scheduled to call at the port of Cobh on the south coast of Ireland. There Peter would disembark and spend some time visiting his family in Ireland. The next port of call was Southampton, England. From there the liner sailed direct to Hamburg where it was due to arrive on Wednesday 16th March.

Gabriela traveled by train from Köln to Hamburg and was there to greet her aunt and cousins when they arrived in the port. Naturally there was great excitement; especially as it was the first visit by the young people to their mother's homeland. They would have over four weeks holiday before departing once again for Canada. This time all being well, Gabriela would be with them. When all the luggage had been brought ashore and cleared by customs the group went to a restaurant for a meal. Well rested after the meal. They took a taxi to the railway station for the journey to Köln. Margret remarked how much things had changed since her last visit home. There was much checking of passports and other documents by the police and the atmosphere was now more tense. The fact that Germany had taken over control of its neighbour, Austria in mid-March had added to the political tension.

The train made good time and soon they were at the home of Susanna. The meeting between the sisters was very emotional. Gabriela had everything organized for the guests. The luggage was placed in the sleeping quarters and presents given to Susanna and Gabriela. Eva and Michael were keen to see the city where their mother had been born, so Gabriela took them out for a walk while the sisters brought each other up to date on family matters. The following days were busy with sight seeing and visiting relations. The Canadian family was introduced to Ernst who wanted to learn all about life across the ocean. At last the documents for Gabriela were approved by the authorities. She was now free to accompany her aunt and cousins to Canada. Her papers gave her permission for a two year stay, during which she would improve on her language skills and teach the German language to Canadian students. She was requested to learn as much as possible about the political situation there and see if she could make a visit to the United States of America. Gabriela discussed the matter with Ernst, has father and her mother. They agreed that she should appear to follow the instructions given to her by the authorities and send some general details back home.

Ernst and Gabriela did have a few opportunities to be alone and discuss their future; Ernst told her that should the situation in Germany develop along the lines forecast by his father, she should stay in Canada as long as possible. Soon he would be doing his own examinations and then he would have no choice but to join one of the military forces. His first choice would of course be the air force, because of his interest in air craft and it also had so many different sections that would not be involved in active warfare where lives had to be taken without any consideration for the ordinary people. He assured Gabriela that he would keep in regular contact with her mother and look after her little dog – Rex. When communicating with each other they would use the name of the dog as a code word when any sensitive details were to be exchanged.

Soon the time of parting came, Ernst traveled with the group to Hamburg where they would join the liner on Wednesday 13th April for the Trans-Atlantic voyage. Once again the family was subject to severe scrutiny by the police and emigration officials. It was with some relief that they eventually boarded the ship. Ernst and Gabriela now had the understanding that when the difficult situation had resolved itself that they would get married and have a home of their own. It was a sad young man who waited by the quayside as the great liner was taken from the harbour by tug boats. He watched the vessel until it was no longer in sight before making his way to the train station for the journey home.

Chapter 4

The Final Examinations

When Ernst returned to Pulheim he was naturally sad and lonesome, but soon he had to return to his studies in the college. As he no longer had Gabriela to spend time with he decided to sign up for advanced photography classes at the college in the evenings. There were some amazing developments in cameras both in new equipment and technology particularly with regard to aerial photography. This would be a great advantage to Ernst if he was successful in his application to join the air force.

With his engineering classes, helping in the family factory, making deliveries of parts to the air field and visits to the swimming pool where he became a proficient swimmer, he had very little spare time. He made many good friends at the air field and on a number of occasions a friendly pilot would take him on short test flights. If the plane had dual controls the pilot would let him fly the air craft. It soon became obvious that he had a natural talent for flying. As these flights had no official standing, one of his friends was instrumental in getting Ernst to join the flying club at the air field and so have his flying hours recorded. He was now making excellent progress in the engineering class. That coupled with assisting his father in making actual parts for planes gave him a great understanding of the mechanical works of planes and of their design.

Observing take-offs and landings regularly gave him room for thought, especially with regard to landing. He noticed that often in landing the planes would bounce with the result that the wheels of the undercarriage would lose contact with the runway. The effect of the brakes was reduced and it took a longer distance to bring the plane to a stop, tyre wear was also increased. Ernst discussed the problem with the pilots and engineers at the air field, with his instructors in the college and with his father. He did much research and decided to make the problem the principal subject for his final examinations which were scheduled to take place in the autumn of 1938. Immediately after this he would have to volunteer to join one of the military forces. He knew that if he volunteered he would have a choice of the air force, whereas if he waited until he was conscripted he could be sent to the army or navy

Meanwhile he had received a letter from Gabriela telling of her safe arrival in Toronto. Her words were carefully chosen as she knew all correspondence passed through the censorship authorities. Along with her cousins she had explored the huge ship. Of course where were sections of the vessel that ordinary passengers were not permitted to go to. She described the family being re-united with Peter O'Reilly when he re-joined the liner at Cobh in Ireland. As much as she would have liked to, Gabriela could not go ashore in Ireland. Deep sea vessels could not dock at Cobh harbour, so a tender was used to bring passengers and goods to the ship which was anchored some distance off shore.

The voyage westwards was uneventful and pleasant; soon they had entered the port of Halifax. Peter pointed out to Gabriela many places of interest: Newfoundland, Prince

Edward Island and Nova Scotia; which means New Scotland, all places where immigrants from Scotland and Ireland had settled over the centuries. As they traveled on the train to the west it was with sadness that Peter described to her the terrible history of the Gross Ile on the St. Lawrence River, which had been a quarantine station for the thousands of Irish men, women and children who had fled from Ireland during the Great Famine in 1845. It was by this route that Peter's own ancestors first came to Canada. Over 8,000 Irish people were buried on this island; many more died on the dreaded coffin ships and were buried at sea. Soon they had passed through the great canal that joined the St. Laurence to Lake Ontario and in a short time they had tied up at the docks in Toronto. It was a happy but tired group of travelers who arrived at the O'Reilly home on the outskirts of the city.

Ernst was now concentrating on his studies and during breaks he would visit Susanna and take Rex for a walk and some exercise in the park. He would also get the latest news from Gabriela in Toronto. Her mother missed her very much, but as she watched the political situation develop in Germany she knew that the right decision had been made for Gabriela to join her aunt in Canada. Ernst with his ideas in mind for a better suspension system for the undercarriage of aero-planes carried out a lot of research into systems used in motorcars and motorcycles. The old methods were becoming outdated, a telescopic hydraulic type of shock absorber was becoming exceedingly popular, but it was still in the early stages of development. The fixed undercarriage was no longer adequate for modern planes, which of course had now become larger and faster. The main landing wheels required a spring system and a method of retracting the undercarriage into the fuselage when the plane was in flight.

A variety of model undercarriage struts were built; tested and rejected, until finally a unique method of shock absorption was devised. It was named the Ringfeder. The strut housed a large number of spring steel chamfered cone shaped rings which fitted into each other in the oil filled strut. On landing the rings took the shock of contact with the ground and the upward bounce was cushioned by friction as the rings separated. Finally the system devised by Ernst in conjunction with his college lecturers, his father and the engineering staff at the air field was ready to be tested. A prototype was built, fitted to a plane and watched by some of the senior Luftwaffe officers as it went through a series of tests. There were several adjustments to be made to the system before it got the full approval of the authorities. Another major modification was made to the wheels of the plane. This took the form of a disk braking system which was a far superior method to the old brakes. When tested in conjunction with the new undercarriage, pilots found that landing an aircraft had become more proficient and safer. Under normal conditions much shorter runway length was needed.

Ernst took his examinations in early autumn of 1938; his work on the new suspension strut was the principal feature of his examination paper. He was required to have a full knowledge of the composition of all types of metals including steel, copper, brass and aluminum. The subject of mathematics was essential for mechanical drawing and design. There was a considerable time lapse before the results of his exam would be given. When not assisting his father in the business, he availed of his free days to take flying lessons at the air field. There the club had bought one of the most modern training planes. It was an Arado twin seat plane fitted with an Argus AS 410 12 cylinder air cooled 450 hp engine. It had a top speed of 211 miles per hour and a range of 615 miles. With a closed in cockpit it could reach a height of 23,000 feet. Ernst built up his flying hours and had an excellent instructor. After some months with many landings and take off's his instructor decided that it was time for him to make his first solo flight.

This flight was of a short duration, just about 20 minutes and it went well for him. Within a few days Ernst had another flight with his instructor. This involved, taking off into the wind, medium turns, powered approaches and landings, followed by gliding approaches and landings. The instructor was pleased with his progress and gave him every opportunity to take solo flights and build up his flying hours. Now that his education course was complete, he had to wait for his exam results. Ernst thought it better at this stage to apply to join the Luftwaffe. He was soon called for interview and there he was closely questioned about his ambition to become a pilot. He had with him his log book that gave all the details of his flying experience and a report from his instructor. His engineering experience was of great interest to the officer doing the interview, as was the work carried out by himself and his father in developing the advanced landing gear strut for air craft. Ernst was asked to return in a few weeks at the end of October 1938 when he had received his examination results.

Chapter 5

A Luftwaffe Pilot

Ernst received his results from the college and he was delighted to find that he had come in at the top of his class; all his hard work and study had brought an excellent result. He had also taken a less difficult examination in photography; and again acquired a better than average mark in the subject. During this time he had regular communication from Gabriela who had settled well to life in Canada. He met at least once a week with Susanna and they exchanged the news from Canada. He always got a great welcome from Rex and took the dog for its usual walk in the park. Ernst realized that when he joined the air force that his correspondence with Gabriela would have to be very discreet due to the fact that all letters to a foreign land would be subject to censorship.

Early in November Ernst received a notice to present himself for a further interview and medical examination at the local headquarters of the Luftwaffe. The officers carrying out the interview were impressed with his examination results both in engineering and photography. They were aware of the work carried out by him and his father in the development of the new struts in the undercarriage that was now being tested with a view to having it used in larger air craft. He was closely questioned about his ongoing flying lessons and his knowledge of air craft in general. Soon he received the word that he had been accepted into the Luftwaffe and ordered to present himself to the local headquarters. The early weeks were spent in training, drilling and attending lectures and learning the routine of being a member of a large group within a military force. After over six weeks of training, he passed all tests with high honour's. Then he was transferred to an elementary flying training school. His previous experience in the flying club was a great advantage and Ernst made a good impression on his instructor as he built up his flying hours both under instruction and in solo flights. He made excellent progress in his training and was then chosen to do a special course in navigation, this being an important aspect for a pilot of an aircraft.

At the end of his training Ernst was one of a small group of pilots selected to progress on to multi-engine aero-planes. As well as learning all about the larger air craft he continued with the advanced course in navigation. This consisted of map reading, the art of dead reckoning navigation, the use of compasses, flying by instruments, reconnaissance, direction finding, night flying and photography. Ernst passed all of these examinations with distinction, this coupled with his actual flying experience meant that he was promoted to the rank of flight sergeant. The Commander of the Group was Colonel Karl Bohmer, a veteran of the Great War and an experienced aviator. The Colonel wore with pride the Knights Cross, first class with Oak Leaves. Very soon he judged Ernst to be exceptional pilot material and took a keen interest in his training. From his observations and listening to remarks made by the Colonel, Ernst came to the conclusion that his commanding officer was not a member of the ruling Nazi party. A man who loved his country and with a checkered history in the Luftwaffe he had decided for himself that he did not need to be a party member to serve his fatherland. Many of the new pilots were party members, but others had resisted pressure to join. The Colonel had made his own judgment of Ernst and while never mentioning the subject he guided Ernst along a safe path. For he knew that this outstanding student with exceptional skills could remain above party politics.

At this time there was great advancement being made in the development of aircraft. One of the greatest aircraft of the period was the new Junkers 88. It was to become an excellent aircraft that could be adapted to any imaginable role. In the late spring of 1939 three of these planes were allocated to the group that Ernst was serving with. The Colonel decided that his best pilots would receive special training and instruction on the Junkers 88. Ernst was one of those chosen to train in one of the new planes. For a large and well built machine its maneuverability was really astonishing. Even with one of its two engines shut off it could fly perfectly under normal circumstances. Its remarkable landing gear was that which had been developed by Ernst and his father. It also had the very powerful disk braking system which made it a pleasure to land on any surface.

The greatest thing about the Junkers 88 was its versatility; it could be used as a bomber, a fighter and as a long range reconnaissance plane for aerial photography. It was possible to fit extra fuel tanks in the bomb bays and so increase the range of the plane to almost 1100 miles. The plane could reach a height if over 26,000 feet and had a top speed of 280 miles per hour. There is no doubt but that the Junkers 88 was one of the most advanced planes of the era. Colonel Bohmer had one of his planes specially fitted out for reconnaissance and photography, Ernst was assigned to this plane and with a carefully selected crew they flew together and practiced their skills to near perfection.

Chapter 6

Gabriela settles in Canada

Gabriela soon settled into the O'Reilly home on the outskirts of Toronto. The house, although old was most spacious. It was situated in a quiet residential district, had a garage and a large cellar, Gabriela had a bedroom of her own on the top floor and a smaller room to use as a study. Her cousins also had rooms of their own where they could do their work from school. At weekends the family would take Gabriela for drives in their car around the country. For her the most wonderful trip of all was the one to the world famous Niagara Falls which are situated between Lake Erie and Lake Ontario. Coming from Germany where the principal waterways were the Rhine and Ruhr and just a few small lakes, Gabriela was impressed with the size of the Canadian lakes.

After a few weeks Gabriela found a position with a language school in Toronto city. Peter was a senior fire officer in one of the large city fire houses; Margret was a secretary with a leading insurance company. Both of them traveled daily to their work by car and so they could bring Gabriela with them. Peter has many connections with in the large Irish community in the city and it had been through some of his influential friends that he got the job for his wife's niece. There was also a sizable German community in Toronto and Margret had good friends amongst them. Some of them were Jews who had escaped from their home land and persecution from the Nazis. In her spare time Gabriela taught them English and they became quite proficient speakers. This meant that they could broaden their scope in seeking employment.

She got on very well with her cousins Eva and Michael and often assisted them with their studies. She also could take charge of the children and the house when the parents would take a short holiday. Gabriela wrote every week to her mother and in return she received all the news from home. In the short time since she had left Germany the political situation had become more difficult. Her mother had to be guarded in what she wrote in the letters, but from the news in the papers and on the radio Gabriela had a good knowledge of how things were at home. Letters between her and Ernst had to be even more discreet. Often their messages to each other were contained in the letters to her mother.

In spite of all this Gabriela was very happy in Canada even though she missed her family and her country. Peter arranged for her to take driving lessons and soon she acquired a full driver's license, this meant that she could help Peter and Margret by doing trips for them. With the coming of winter and the heavy snowfalls Gabriela was amazed with the change in the country. Nevertheless she adapted very well and soon got used to this new way of life. The old year of 1938 passed by and the New Year of 1939 got under way. As the months passed by it became evident that the situation in Europe was becoming more serious and that there was danger of a war breaking out. This was a cause of great worry to the young German girl and she feared for the safety of her mother and of Ernst who by this time had become a member of the Luftwaffe and was training to be a pilot. Gabriela made excellent progress in the language school with the result that she got promotion to higher grades with more responsibilities and higher wages. She contributed to the upkeep of the O'Reilly home and on occasion could send some money back to her mother.

Chapter 7

Ernst becomes a pilot

Under the guidance of Colonel Bohmer who had taken a special interest in Ernst, the young man made great progress in his chosen branch of the service. No one only he and a specially selected crew were permitted to fly the Junkers 88 which was one of the most up to date aircraft in the unit. It was specially fitted with modern photography equipment and reconnaissance instruments. For long range missions it had extra fuel tanks fitted in the bomb bays. Appointed to the crew as a pilot/ navigator/flight engineer were Sergeant Paul Lehmann, photographer/air gunner – Sergeant Gerhardt Distler and a meteorologist, Arthur Niemann who was not a member of the air force but a talented civilian who would carry out his professional duties aboard the aircraft.

The four men trained together and flew on many missions, some to Poland and other eastern European countries, others to France and the low lands. When Ernst had built up his flying hours and gained invaluable experience he was promoted to Leutenant. The four men of the crew of this special Junkers plane became firm friends, understanding each other and helping each other at all times. It was fortunate that none of them belonged to the ruling Nazi party and due to the strong influence of Colonel Bohmer they were not put under any pressure to join the party. He maintained that there was no question of their loyalty to their country and that their specialized duties were of the utmost important to the Luftwaffe.

When as expected, war broke out in 1939 Ernst and his crew had become one of the most experienced units in their department of the Luftwaffe. The Colonel ensured that they never took part in any belligerent missions and so avoided any engagement with enemy aircraft. After the German invasion of Poland, Britain and France entered the war. In a short time Belgium, Holland and France fell to the German land forces. The Luftwaffe established new airfields in western France and it was one of these that Ernst and his crew were transferred to in the 1940's. From there they flew on meteorological missions out over the Atlantic Ocean and on photographic missions over England, Wales and Scotland. They were also sent on fights over the neutral Irish Free State and as far north as Northern Ireland on reconnaissance and photographic missions.

With Canada being part of the Commonwealth and now in the war both Ernst and Gabriela accepted that it would no longer be possible to communicate with each other as all their letters would be censored and read. Messages could be passed through Susanna as long as mail was being delivered between Germany and Canada. Ernst was held in high esteem by his commanding officer and soon he was promoted to the rank of Captain. His comrades Paul Lehmann and Gerhardt Distler were promoted to be Leutenants. The civilian crew member Herr Arthur Niemann received a suitable honour in keeping with his status in his profession.

As the war progressed Hitler prepared plans for the invasion of the island of Ireland. Following the fight for independence from England in the 1920's the country was divided into two portions. The six north eastern counties remained as part of the United Kingdom and under British rule. The remaining twenty six counties became an independent country known as The Irish Free State or Eire. The new state had declared a policy of strict neutrality and did not become involved in the war. Two plans to invade Ireland were prepared; one named 'Plan Cathleen' was for the invasion of the Free State, the other named 'The Green Plan' was for the invasion of the six counties of Northern Ireland. Should the invasion plans have been put into operation, Ireland had neither the arms nor equipment to deal with such a situation. The country would have been overrun in a few days thus leaving the west coast of Britain open to an invasion. Although not aware of these plans, Ernst and his crew were ordered to carry out an extensive photographic survey of what was known in Germany as The Green Isle.

The Junkers 88 was fitted out with the most up to date navigational and photographic equipment, all of which was very top secret. Ernst and his crew were under strict orders that in the event of the plane crashing it was to be destroyed by explosion and fire to prevent this equipment falling into enemy hands. The bomb bays in the plane were fitted with extra fuel tanks so as to increase the range of the air craft. A small number of explosive and incendiary bombs were carried for use in an emergency. A number of German intelligence agents had been placed in Ireland. Some of them landed by parachute, others came ashore from U-Boats. As in any country which is composed of a mainly rural community any foreign person was seen as being out of place. So intelligence agents were soon found and arrested to be interned in a prison of war camp.

Many missions were flown by this experienced crew and their special air craft. The weather along the east coast of the Atlantic was unpredictable and often not suited for photography. Particular attention was paid to the border between the Irish Free State and Northern Ireland. Ernst developed a particular personal interest in Ireland as it was from this country that the husband of Gabriela's aunt came. He managed to build up a personal folio of photographs of Ireland and this he carried with him on his missions. Particular attention had to be paid to the Northern Ireland city of Belfast for there was situated the world famous shipyards of Harland and Wolf. Also in the city there were factories for the building of aircraft and the manufacture of vital military equipment. It became an important port for the importation of supplies brought by the shipping convoys from the United States of America and Canada.

There was considerable danger for Ernst and his crew for they would be subject to attack from British fighter planes and from anti-aircraft guns. They had several narrow escapes, using superior speed and altitude to avoid detection. As he became more and more familiar with the landscape and with the coast line, Ernst formulated several plans to be used in the event of an emergency caused by either an attack from the enemy or from a mechanical failure in his plane. In early 1941 the photographs taken showed some unusual activity taking place on the large lake named Lough Erne in the County of Fermanagh, Northern Ireland. On several of his missions Ernst was instructed to pay particular attention to this area.

Lough Erne was situated quite close to the west coast of Ireland and the Atlantic Ocean where shipping convoys brought supplies to Britain from Canada and the United States of America. As there were no fighter planes or other means of defense in this part of Ireland, Ernst was able to fly at a low altitude and so he became very familiar with the landscape and the layout of the country. He noted how the lake became a river before entering the Atlantic at the coast. He knew what towns and villages were in Northern Ireland, which were part of the United Kingdom and therefore at war with Germany. He knew which were in the neutral Free State where there were no black out regulations, whereas in Northern Ireland it was serious offence to let lights be seen after night fall. He became familiar with the mountain areas, flat areas and the smaller lakes near the border.

There were few opportunities for Ernst to get home to visit his parents. The city of Köln had in early 1941 become a prime target for British bombers and so was a most dangerous place to live. On one of his rare visits home Ernst and his parents decided to invite Susanna to move from her apartment in the city and live in Pulheim where there was less danger of suffering damage from bomb raids. This she agreed to and with the help of Dieter and Ernst all her belongings were transported to a suitable apartment near the Schmitt home. Correspondence between Susanna and Gabriela was now uncertain; still they managed to get word to Canada about the change of residence.

The missions that Ernst had to fly on were becoming more and more dangerous. If his flight path was some where between Britain and Ireland, he was within range of allied fighter planes. If he flew over neutral Ireland, protests were made to the German Legation in Dublin. Many times he had to fly westwards out into the Atlantic and turn eastwards to get over Northern Ireland. Ernst and his crew made a number of photographic flights over Belfast city in the spring of 1941. As a result of the information gained from the photographs a small squadron of German bombers led by a Heinkel pathfinder carried out a raid on Belfast on the night of the 7th of April. A large portion of the Harland and Wolf shipyards and air craft factory was destroyed as was a major timber yard and a section of the docks. Belfast was very poorly defended and the German squadron suffered no losses.

Some days after the blitz of Belfast Colonel Bohmer invited Ernst into his office and said that he had a special mission of great importance for him. He said that the German high command were not satisfied with the raid on Belfast and felt that several important targets had escaped damage. He instructed Ernst to carry out a photographic mission to Belfast and pay particular attention to the docks area and to the ship building yards of Harland and Wolf. The pictures would have to be taken at a low level and in daylight. Following a long discussion and the examination of photographs taken by Ernst and his crew prior to the blitz it was decided that late evening was the best time to fly over the city. It would also be necessary to have a good amount of cloud to escape into as it was most likely that there would be anti-aircraft fire and possibly fighter planes in the air. As this was solely a reconnaissance mission it was not necessary to bring along Arthur Niemann the meteorologist. On Thursday 10th of April the Junkers aircraft was fully prepared for the flight. The large extra fuel tanks were put in place in the bomb bay; there was still space for two small explosive bombs and several incendiary bombs. All equipment was fully checked out including the cameras, machine guns and emergency gear. The Colonel briefed the crew and stressed the importance of the mission and the dangers that they would be faced with. There must be no danger of the highly sophisticated and secret equipment falling into enemy hands. The flight plan was discussed and it was decided to take a westerly course from France out over the Atlantic, then northwards along the west coast of Ireland and turning inland when in line with Belfast. This would entail flying at a high altitude across neutral Ireland and approaching the target area from the west. The part of Northern Ireland that they would fly over was poorly defended and hopefully the authorities in Belfast would not expect a German plane to come from this direction.

In the late evening Ernst made his approach to the city of Belfast, he descended below the cloud level and flew along the Lagan River; he instructed Gerhardt to get the cameras in motion and held a steady course towards the dock area where the ship building yards and aircraft factories were situated. He was rather surprised to see that the damage was not quite as serious as had been reported by the bomber crews. What did concern him was the fact that there was much destruction in the residential part of Belfast. Once out over Belfast Lough he turned around round to pass over the city again instructing Gerhard to photograph the many wrecked homes. As he finished this pass his plane was attacked by a Hurricane fighter plane that had suddenly appeared out of the low cloud. Ernst took evasive action but unfortunately the Junkers was hit by the enemy gunfire taking several hits. He immediately increased to full speed and climbed into the cloud to get away from the Hurricane as it swept around to make a second attack. He was lucky to escape from the enemy plane.

Knowing that his plane had taken several hits he asked Paul to access the situation. Paul left the co-pilots seat and went down to the position occupied by Gerhardt. He was shocked to discover that his comrade had taken a direct hit from the Hurricane guns and had lost his life. Returning to the flight deck he reported the sad news to Ernst. The plane was answering to all controls and at first did not seem to suffer any serious damage. But on checking the instruments Paul discovered that the temperature of the starboard engine has risen to a very high level. A further check showed that the cooling supply tank to the engine had been ruptured by the machine gun bullets. The temperature of the engine had risen to an alarming level so there was no alternative to shutting down the engine and feathering the propeller. Ernst and Paul discussed the seriousness of their situation and realized that there was no possibility of returning to base with the damaged air craft. They continued flying in a westward direction with the intention of reaching the Irish coast and ditching the Junkers in the ocean where its secret equipment would not fall into the hands of the enemy. Paul managed to send a brief radio message to base stating that following an attack by an enemy fighter plane they were preparing to ditch the Junkers.

After about thirty minutes flying time darkness had fallen but there was clear moonlight that gave some visibility. The two men gave some serious consideration to their predicament; there was no sign of any pursuit by enemy aircraft who probably assumed that the Junkers would have taken the direct route southwards in an attempt to reach their home base. Now being in familiar territory Ernst and Paul hit on a daring plan that might save their plane from capture by the British authorities and enable the two men to reach the safety of the neutral Free State.

Chapter 8

Ditching in a Mountain Lake

Ernst had the maps of the area and a number of the photographs that they had taken on earlier missions. He asked Paul to find these so they could study them and plan a course of action. The Junkers handled reasonably well on one engine, but there was always the danger that if anything went wrong with it the situation would be out of their control and they might crash on land. They were lucky that along the westward route they were following there were no fighter plane bases or anti-aircraft guns. They were now clear of cloud and visibility was reasonably good in the moon light. Ernst on checking the maps could see that on their route was a fairly high cone shaped hill which was a good land mark. To reach this land mark they had to keep clear of Lough Erne as their previous missions had shown that this was being used as a base for flying boats. They kept a safe distance north of the lake before resuming the search for the hill which was their land mark. To the south of this hill there was a very expansive area of fairly flat moorland and it was close to the border between Northern Ireland and the Free State. To the northeast of the hill and the flat area, were two reasonable sized lakes in a remote area.

It was imperative that the plane and its valuable secret equipment should not fall into the hands of the enemy. At this stage of the war there was every indication that Germany would be victorious. Ernst and Paul wanted if possible to ditch the Junkers in a place from which it could be recovered, rather than put it down in the Atlantic Ocean off the west coast of Ireland. Checking the land maps they could see that just on the border there were two lakes. One was almost the shape of the letter 'C' and almost wholly in the Irish Free State, the second lake was more of an oblong shape and about half and half on each side of the border. The copy of the map that they had; showed that it was of a reasonable enough size and depth to ditch an aircraft into and it could remain hidden from view. The two men devised a plan that they hoped would be successful to keep the location of the plane a secret. If all went well they would make their way across the border into the Free State. First they would fly over the large expanse of flat moor land and jettison the two extra fuel tanks stored in the bomb bay. Both still contained a considerable amount of fuel. They would then do a

circle and drop both explosive and incendiary bombs near the fuel tanks. This would create a large explosion, ignite the fuel and give the impression to people in the locality that the plane they would have heard flying over head would have crashed on the moor.

The next stage of the operation would be most tricky and require the skill of both pilots. With Ernst at the controls the tanks were dropped as planned and when the bombs were dropped there was a huge explosion and in a short time the surface of the moor was ablaze. Immediately this happened Ernst cut out the remaining engine, set the plane on an angled dive to reach the lake which was at least a mile from the scene of the fire. This exercise was carried out in complete silence and by using the efficient air brakes Ernst brought the plane down on the surface of the lake just before it had reached stalling speed. The bomb bay doors were left open, the undercarriage was put into the down position and all hatches opened so that the plane would take in plenty of water and sink beneath the surface. Paul had the small inflatable dinghy ready at the entrance hatch, for the plane would not sink immediately. All went according to plan and soon the Junkers had settled on the surface of the lake and was slowly starting to sink. One problem remained. What would they do about the body of their dead comrade – Gerhardt? With what little time they had left they moved his body close to the flight deck entrance and secured it to the frame of the plane in case that it should become free and float to the surface. They got the dinghy inflated and paddled clear of the plane as it sank beneath the surface without trace. It would rest in over thirty feet of water on the bed of the lake. As they made their way to the west shore and to the Irish Free State they could see the glow on the sky line of the still burning moor land.

Reaching the shore the two men deflated the dinghy, rolled it into as small a bundle as possible and bound it with the ropes that were attached to it. Using the paddles as tools they dug a trench in the soft peat bed of the lake, placed the dinghy in it and covered it with stones that were on the shore. Now all evidence of the men and their plane was hidden from view. Keeping a careful lookout they made their way to a small country road that led into the Free State of Ireland. It was now almost midnight and having crossed the border the men could see a dull light in a small farm house on a hill side. As they came near the house a dog started to bark and raised an alarm. The door was opened and out came the owner. He bid the dog to be quiet saying, "Down, Sport, be quiet". The well-built elderly farmer then spotted the two men in the strange uniforms. He told them not to be alarmed, assuring them that they were in safe hands. He invited them into the house and secured the door. Living so close to the border; it was not an unusual occurrence to have strangers calling to his home.

Having heard the noise of a plane and the explosion near Breesy Hill he had judged that the callers were from the plane. Asking them did they understand the English language, Ernst assured them that they both did, although he would be more proficient than his comrade. The man of the house then introduced himself, "My name is Dan Mooney and I live alone here on this small farm. I take it that you are Germans and that you are from the plane that I heard fly around here several times tonight. I then heard a loud explosion followed by a large fire out in the Croagh near Breesy Mountain. You have nothing to fear from me and you are welcome to stay with me until such times as you make plans about your future". Dan bid the two men to remove their wet and muddy clothing and gave them some of his own clothes to wear until their own had dried out. Guessing that the men were hungry he stroked up the open hearth fire and added more turf to it. He filled up the kettle and from a container on the dresser he produced some cold meat and bacon. He then selected a few fresh hen eggs which he placed in a small saucepan and set it on the fire to boil. He set the big wooden kitchen table with three large mugs, plates, bread, butter, salt, pepper and jam. By now Ernst and Paul had changed their clothing and felt more comfortable in the heat of the large open fire.

In a short time Dan had a first class meal ready and the three of them sat at the table to enjoy it. As they were eating Ernst introduced himself and Paul, confirming that they were indeed German airmen whose plane he had heard and which had crashed in the locality. Ernst said that their plane was now in such a position that it could not be discovered easily. He assured Dan that although they were members of the Luftwaffe neither Paul nor himself were Nazis, they did not approve of the present leadership in their homeland, but they were compelled by law to be in a military service. After a welcome and enjoyable meal, the table was cleared and the three men sat beside the warm fire to relax and have a smoke of cigarettes provided by Dan. He assured them that they were in the neutral Free State of Ireland and that they were welcome to stay with him until some plan of action was decided on. Dan said that being on the border he had means of providing them with a safe place to remain out of sight when callers would come to his home. Of course there would most likely in the morning be teams of investigators on each side of the border when the police and army got reports of a plane being in the area and of the explosion and fire on the mountain. It being long past midnight Ernst and Paul were very tired and feeling the effects of the experience that they had been through since leaving their base in France the previous day. The house was the traditional Irish thatched farm dwelling with a large open kitchen in the centre and a bedroom at each end. Dan showed the men into one bedroom that had two single beds that they would sleep in. He told them that his dog 'Sport' always remained outside at night and that if anyone came any where near the house he would raise the alarm.

All three men were awake early the next morning and considerably refreshed. Dan advised Ernst and Paul to continue to wear his civilian clothing even if it was not a really good fit for them. It was also better to remain indoors. He prepared them a good breakfast and leaving them in the house he attended the livestock and to his horse. Dan took the opportunity to climb to the top of the hill and survey the district. Very soon he observed a contingent of British military carrying out a search of the Croagh which was in Northern Ireland. On the Free State side of the border two lorry loads of Irish soldiers were also to be seen. Returning to the house Dan made his guests aware of the situation and said that it would not be long until the Irish Military and police would be paying him a visit as his was one of the few houses in the area. This was not an unusual situation for Dan to be in for since the establishment of the border over fifteen years ago his house and farm had received attention from the authorities in their attempts to combat smuggling and that other profession that lay outside the scope of the law on both sides of the border. It being the illegal trade of poteen distilling, the Irish home brewed spirits.

With Sport on guard duty outside, Dan explained the situation to the German airman. The floor of the kitchen was in the tradition Irish style; that is one of large flat flag stones. He brought a small sized milk churn (used to bring milk to the creamery) into the house; he got the two men to place their uniforms and other items inside the churn. When he lifted one of the flag stones there was a hidden square pit to be seen, it already contained several items including a number of bottles. The churn was then placed in the pit and the flag stone replaced, a quick run of a brush sealed up the joints in the stone work. Another surprise was in store for the visitors. Built up outside against the long side wall of the house was a large stack of turf. Inside the kitchen on the same wall was a wooden press reaching to the ceiling. Dan opened the door of the press; at the top of it he removed a steel pin and did the same at the bottom. Then to the amazement of the men the press swung around to reveal an opening in the wall. This led into a small hidden chamber that was about six foot square, inside there was some strange looking equipment that the men were later to learn was a still used in the manufacture of the poteen. All this was concealed by the stack of turf outside the house. Dan explained to the men that when the Irish military and police came to his house, the men would enter the secret chamber and remain concealed there until the danger was past.

He said that the airmen did not have many options, one being to remain with him until some plan of action could be worked out. The other was to surrender to the authorities and be interned as prisoners of war for the duration of the conflict. From reading the papers Dan knew that two German planes had already crashed along the south coast of Ireland. One in County Wexford on Monday 3rd March 1941, was a Heinkel bomber. The crew were taken into custody and interned in a prisoner of war camp in the Curragh, Co. Kildare. Another Heinkel had crashed in Waterford on the 1st April and like wise the crew was taken to the Curragh. Having some time to relax and with Sport on guard duty the men sat around the fire side enjoying mugs of tea. Dan said to the Germans, "I am sure you think it strange and unusual that I should offer you the hospitality of my home in your present situation. It will surprise you to learn that I owe my life to a young German soldier. During the last war as a member of the British army I served in France. My regiment the famous Royal Inniskilling Fusiliers was taking part in the third battle of Ypres in November 1917. Along with four comrades I was manning a machine gun nest in the trenches. An enemy shell scored an almost direct hit that killed my friends and left me severely wounded. Knowing that in a short time the Germans would reach the destroyed machine gun nest and shoot any survivors I prepared for the end by taking out my rosary to say some prayers. As expected a young German soldier jumped into the pit with his rifle and bayonet at the ready to finish me off. Had the situation been reversed we would have done the same to a German machine gun crew, that was the cruelties of war. Suddenly he stopped and pointed his rifle towards my rosary, saying in German, "Are you Catholic"? I answered, "Yes, I am Catholic and from Ireland". He immediately put down his gun, took a first aid kit from his haversack, cut away the sleeve of my tunic and bandaged my wound.

Dan continued with this remarkable story, telling how the young soldier escorted him to the first aid post at his head quarters. There a doctor treated the wound and he was sent to a hospital. When he had recovered he was then taken to a prisoner of war camp and interned until the war was over. Dan continued, "Now I have the chance to repay the kindness shown to me many years ago by a young countryman of yours. I am prepared to do every thing possible to help you in your present situation. It is better that I do not know where you have disposed of your aero plane, for if I should be questioned I can truthfully say that I have no knowledge of it". Having listened to this remarkable story Ernst and Paul were confident that here was a man that they could trust. Ernst then said to Dan, "Thank you, for your kindness to us both. We have a problem that we will need your help with; there was one other member of our crew who lost his life when we were attached near Belfast by a British fighter plane. His name was Gerhardt Distler. One of the engines was so badly damaged that it was impossible for us to return to our base on France. So we had no alternative but to ditch our plane. Sadly his body is still aboard the plane". Ernst went on to explain that their mission was a photographic one and not a bombing one that would have resulted in a loss of life. Dan said that he was sorry to learn about the death of their comrade but that they would wait for some days until the authorities had finished their search of the district. If Gerhardt's body could be recovered they would work out a plan to have him buried with dignity and respect.

Ernst and Paul had to remain indoors during the day, but at night Dan took them out for trips around his farm so that they could get some exercise and relief from boredom. On the afternoon of the third day after the crash of the plane, Sport started to bark in an excited manner. Looking out Dan could see Garda Sergeant Tom O'Sullivan crossing the fields accompanied by a contingent of Irish soldiers. Quickly he ushered the two men into the hidden room and had the wooden press back in place before the Sergeant arrived at the door. The bedroom door was open and as they had done each morning, the beds were made up and tidy giving no indication that they had recently been slept in. Dan bade Sport to stop his barking and invited the sergeant into the house. After the usual exchange of pleasantries the question came up about the explosion on the Croagh. Dan said that he had indeed heard the noise of an aircraft on the night in question, but the noise ceased after the explosion and fire. He said that since the establishment of the air bases on nearby Lough Erne it was no longer a novelty to hear the noise of planes flying overhead both during the day and at night. Dan gave his opinion that if a plane passed to the other side of Breesy Mountain he would no longer hear it. While the men were talking in the house the military had a good look around the farmyard and examined the inside of the out offices. Throughout all this Dan was very relaxed and composed; giving no indication that anything unusual had occurred. He stated that as the Croagh was a considerable distance from his house he had no occasion to go there. He assured Sergeant O'Sullivan that if he would see anything out of the ordinary that he would let him know. The sergeant told Dan that they had searched all around Breesy and sent some men to the summit to survey the surrounding area. They found nothing apart from seeing the large area of gorse and heather that had been burned on the Croagh. There was no evidence to indicate that a plane may have crashed in the area.

The Sergeant was well aware that Dan, who was involved in smuggling and poteen making, would not want the forces of law and order spending too much time in the area.

Dan had always chosen to work alone and was most discreet about this part of his life; he never created any problems for the authorities who turned a blind eye on his activities. Shortly after the contingent had departed and the coast was clear, Dan let his guests out of the secret room and they all sat down to talk and relax. Ernst and Paul were amazed at the manner in which Dan had handled the whole situation and his attitude towards the police and army. They said that in Germany the police and military dealt with the people in a very strict and regimental way. In a similar situation in their country Dan would have been handled in a severe way, held at gun point, undergone intense questioning while the house and building under went a most thorough search.

Dan expected that soon the search of the Croagh would be completed by the authorities from Northern Ireland as it was within their jurisdiction. From a vantage point on the hilltop the three men could observe the proceedings. They talked about many things including the situation in Germany. Ernst told about his fiancée – Gabriela – having gone with her aunt to Canada and that she would be safe there for the duration of the war. He was naturally worried about the safety of his parents and of Susanna the mother of Gabriella. Dan explained how he, an Irishman had come to join the British army in 1914; a small rural farm could not provide an income for the members of his family. The army provided him with a wage and part of his income went to his parents to support his younger brothers and sisters. Because of the injuries he had received on the front he had been awarded a small disability pension that enabled him to live in reasonable comfort on the small farm. His brothers and sisters now lived in different parts of the world; some in Dublin; others in the United States, England and Canada.

There being no road within reasonable distance of the Croagh the search party would have to travel for a considerable distance over a soft and rugged terrain. (There were no helicopters in those times). About ten Royal Air Force personnel were accompanied by several policemen from Northern Ireland who would be familiar with the exact layout of the border. Dan, Ernst and Paul were able to observe the proceedings from their vantage point on the hill. After some time the made their way back to the house, hidden from view by a high hedge. The search party withdrew in the evening without appearing to have discovered anything. At the evening meal there was the chance to talk over some plan of action. Dan said that the following day he would have to go to the nearby village of Belleek where the monthly fair was being held. He would as he normally did bring a cart of turf to sell to one of his customers in the village. The men would give him a hand to fill up the cart in the evening after dark. Before loading on the turf, Dan removed a board from the bed of the cart; this revealed a long narrow compartment. Into this he placed several bottles of a clear liquid, similar to the German Schnapps. The bottles were secured by loose hay and the board replaced. Dan warned the airmen that they should remain indoors while Sport would be as alert as ever in the farmyard. At any sign of danger the front door should be locked from the inside with a spare key, Ernst and Paul would then take up their place in the hidden room. The entrance could be secured from the inside by two bolts. As things turned out there was no alarm and it was not necessary to take any action. Dan had a good collection of books, magazines and old newspapers; this kept the men occupied during the day.

Chapter 9

Planning an escape

As Dan made an early start to the village cattle fair, he gave deep thought to find some way to help Ernst and Paul. At the moment the primary requirement was to obtain civilian clothing for the men, due to the war time rationing the required items could only be purchased in Northern Ireland with government coupons. It would not be possible for a single person to have enough coupons for this purpose. In any case as Dan lived in the Free State he would not have any ration coupons for Northern Ireland and even if he could get some on the Black Market, to make such a purchase it would only attract a considerable amount of unnecessary attention. There was a way to get around this dilemma, on every fair day there would be a number of traders selling all sorts of secondhand items from their stalls. Those who sold clothing were known as 'Cant men'. The more respectable of these dealers had good stocks of nearly new suits, overcoats, shirts and so on. Their goods could be sold on the market without any rationing restrictions. When Dan had sold his cart load of turf, he then took his bottles of poteen from their hiding place and put them into the pockets of his clothing, put on his large overcoat leaving it open so it was not obvious that he was carrying anything. There were several policemen on duty as was usual on a fair day, Dan had taken his horse out of the cart and put it into the yard of a friend with a bag of hay at its head. He waited until the police patrol went down the street towards the border before making his way to a public house where he had a buyer for the bottles of the 'Mountain Dew', the name by which the illegal brew was known.

Having sold all his wares and with a few pounds in his pocket Dan went first to one of the local 'eating houses' for a meal. Next he visited the grocery and hardware store, where he made some necessary purchases of items that were not rationed. He wandered up and down the street having the occasional conversation with neighbours and friends from around the area. Now and again he stopped to have a yarn with the Cant men, observing their wares. He had a good idea of the sizes that would be suitable; in one stall there was a navy blue double breasted three piece suit that would be ideal for Ernst. He examined it without showing too much interest. As was the custom, the dealer hoping for a sale started his talk describing the suit as if was the best one ever made. He insisted on Dan taking off his overcoat and jacket and fitting on the one that was for sale. It was a reasonable fit, but Dan gave a show of reluctance to buy it. Then the haggling commenced. The offer had of course to be less that the asking price. Lookers on, anxious to assist with the deal got involved and soon hands were slapped and the sale was completed. The suit was folded up, wrapped in a newspaper and tied with string and Dan set off along the street. He had spotted several pairs of shoes on the stall and turning back he said that he would buy a pair of shoes if they were to come at the right price. He and the dealer selected a nice pair of black shoes and agreed on a price; Dan said he would pay the price if he was given a pair of socks into the bargain. So the deal was completed and a happy man set of to leave the purchases in his cart.

Next he had to find something for Paul. He went to another stall that was a good distance from the first one, for to buy all his requirements from one dealer would probably have attracted unnecessary attention. On one stall he spotted a very elegant looking black suit. An idea was forming in his mind. A son of his eldest sister who lived in Dublin was a priest in a Missionary Order. Father John Bourke would occasionally travel from Dublin to Donegal on a visit to his uncle. Dan examined several of the suits on display on the stall. Soon the crafty stall holder engaged him in conversation enquiring what he might be on the lookout for. The trader was very anxious to sell the black suit saying that it had belonged to a priest who had died recently in a parish in the next county. It was tailor made and of excellent quality, Dan said that he would be the laughing stock of the country if he went about dressed as a priest. Knowing that here was a bargain judging by the asking price, he said maybe if you sell me the trousers on their own I could wear then working on the land. The dealer said that he could not do that, and so anxious was he to sell that he reduced the price by ten shillings. Wise in the ways of dealing, Dan turned to walk away when a final offer was made, the dealer said that he had a hat and a black shirt to go along with the suit and he would throw them into the bargain and so a sale was completed. The items were wrapped up in a sheet of paper and tied with string and so Dan set off to his cart more than well satisfied with his purchase.

He set off for home in the late afternoon. It was necessary to take a different road home; there were several reasons for this. When he crossed the border near the village he could travel all the way in the Free State and so avoid being stopped and maybe searched by an inquisitive policeman. Also he would pass by a small country grocer shop on his own side of the border where he could purchase food stuff without ration coupons. It was well on in the evening when he reached home, tired and hungry. Sport the dog of course was there to greet him as were Paul and Ernst. The two young men helped him to bring his purchases into the house and when the horse had been attended to they prepared a meal. With Sport on guard duty outside, Dan showed the men what he had bought, explaining that they had to have something to wear instead of their uniforms. They could not be kept hidden indefinitely from prying eyes or casual visitors. Should the occasion arise when some one did call, he would introduce them as nephews of his from Dublin. Ernst was the first to try on his outfit. Though not a perfect fit he looked remarkably well in it. The shoes were a bit large, but some hay stuffed into the toe and an extra pair of socks solved that problem.

Now it was the turn of Paul. Apart from the trousers being a bit wide and long he looked most elegant especially when he donned his hat. He would have passed in most company for a respectable clergyman. Sitting around the turf fire the men discussed various plans of action regarding the future of the airmen. If it became absolutely necessary they could surrender themselves to the Free State authorities. Dan had an idea whereby one of them could make it to Dublin and seek refuge in the German Legation and maybe find passage on an Irish merchant ship to neutral Spain. He explained how his nephew in Dublin was a member of a Missionary Order. Fr. John had worked in the foreign missions for several years until he was forced to return to Ireland when war broke out. He was proficient in several languages including German. As a result he carried out the duties of Chaplain to different foreign groups in Dublin and in the surrounding area. Dan could invite him for a visit to Donegal as he often did, coming by train from Dublin. Paul, dressed as a priest could then accompany Fr. John back to Dublin where he would be safe until a further plan was devised. During these war years clergymen and other members of religious groups could travel with near complete immunity from the authorities. It was left at that and they could think it over, something else would have to be worked out for Ernst. It was now time to retire for the night.

The next morning Dan was attending to his work around the house. The cattle had to be looked after, as had his horse. Shortly before noon the dog Sport gave a few warning barks and was looking towards the border at the bottom of the hill. Dan could see what was annoying Sport. Cycling along the road towards the County Bridge, which was the crossing point over a stream that marked the border, was a police officer. Dan recognized him and said to the two men, "That is Officer Sam Fletcher, a most officious policeman. He has his nose stuck in everything and soft talks local people with a view to getting information from them on smuggling and poteen making. He has a great ambition for promotion in the force. Although this is outside his jurisdiction he often comes to my house for a rest and a mug of tea. So you had better take refuge in the usual place". While Dan stood in the doorway he told the young Germans to watch the procedure through the window. The officer propped his big black bicycle against the wall of the bridge, removed his trouser clips and placed then on the handlebars. Draped over the handlebars and secured with its belt was a civilian gabardine raincoat. The officer put on the coat over his uniform, placed his police cap in the saddlebag of the bike, put on a cloth cap and pushing his machine proceeded up the hill towards Dan's house where he propped it against the wall.

By now the two men had retreated into their place of refuge, Dan told them to listen to the conversation with this unwanted guest. When the officer arrived at the door Dan greeted him in a civil manner that did not reveal his true feelings. "Good morning, officer, to what do I owe this unexpected visit to a foreign land from His Majesty's representative of law and order?" The sarcasm of Dan was lost on the policeman who an Irishman would have described as being thick, meaning he had a density of mind that made him a slow thinker. "Well Mr. Mooney, I have received information from a reliable source that an enemy aircraft may have crashed some where in this district. Knowing that in the past you served in a loyal manner in his Majesty's Royal Inniskilling Fusiliers I considered that you would be a dependable source of information as to what may have happened". Dan said that he had indeed heard an aircraft flying overhead late one night, but as the officer was only to well aware since the establishment of the flying boat bases on Lough Erne planes were flying from there out to the Atlantic Ocean on patrol. Knowing that Officer Fletcher had extreme views on the neutrality of the Free State and its leadership Dan said, "There are strong rumours that the Irish prime Minister – Eamon deValera had given permission to the Churchill led British government to allow the flying boats to fly over a portion of the neutral territory as a way of assisting the Allies in the war." Mention of deValera to Fletcher was like showing a red rag to a bull and as had been Dan's intention the officer had difficulty controlling his temper.

To cool things down somewhat and with a view to keeping the conversation along the same lines, Dan invited the officer to come into his home and join him in a drink of tea. Soon the kettle was boiled and the tea pot filled with a good strong brew. As the men sat at the table drinking from the big mugs, Dan produced a small flat bottle containing some clear liquid. He said that it was good quality poteen and perhaps the officer would like to sample a small portion of it in his tea. The man at first declined, but Dan said that as he was outside his jurisdiction, no harm could be done in having a small sample. Fletcher agreed to the offer and found that it had an agreeable effect on the tea. Dan got the chat going again about the rumoured crash and said that if he found any Germans about the place he would soon sort then out with his double barrel shot gun. He filled up the mugs again with more hot tea and as he did so he poured a liberal dollop of poteen into the policeman's mug.

Dan said to his visitor, "It is a wonder that a fine big strong man like yourself did not join the army and fight for king and country instead of being attached to a police station in this wild part of the country? Would the army not suit you better than traveling over the mountain looking to see if poor farmers were smuggling a few cattle, making a bit of decent poteen or not having a license for a dog or a bull?" Dan had his man upset again as was his intention. The drink was now taking some effect and the policeman said, "I will have you know my good man that in the execution of my duty along this border I can do as much for the defense of the realm as any soldier. It is common knowledge that enemy spies are operating in your Free State". To cool the man down Dan gave him a final mug of tea again with another good share of poteen in it. Finishing his tea the officer said that it was time for him to return to the station and fill in his report on the duties he had carried out during the day. Naturally there would be no mention of his illicit visit across the border; Dan assured him that he would never mention it to a living soul.

Outside the house Fletcher fitted the cycling clips on his trousers, mounted his bike and set off down the steep lane to the road and to the County Bridge. The drink had not yet taken full effect, but from experience Dan knew that when the police man was hit by fresh air everything would change. He let the two Germans out of the hiding place and bid them watch the departing cyclist gather speed as he went down hill. At the bottom he lost all control of the machine, it hit the wall of the bridge and he was catapulted over the handlebars and into the stream. The men watched as he gathered himself up and could hear a litany of curse and swear words from the unfortunate man. Dan produced a set of binoculars and had an excellent view as Fletcher extracted himself from the water and climbed back to the road. Now the drink had taken full effect and he was having difficulty holding an upright position. Dan could see him examine the bicycle. The front tyre was burst, the forks bent and the left hand pedal crank was twisted under the frame leaving it impossible to ride the bike. His uniform trousers were ripped and covered in mud; he removed his gabardine coat, donned his cap and set off staggering along the road supported by the damaged bike. The three men could hear the roars and shouts of the unfortunate victim of the accident until he disappeared from their sight.

Ernst and Paul were not only amazed but delighted at this performance by their host, such treatment of a member of a police force would never be heard tell of in Germany.

Dan said that the man had nobody to blame only himself; his greed did not allow him to refuse a free drink even if it was the illegal poteen. When he eventually made his way back to the Barracks where he was stationed his Sergeant would have something to say to him. Dan had a cousin, Anne McKeany who was cook/housekeeper in the barracks so in time he would hear the full story when the policeman was made to suffer from the consequences of his day on border patrol. Some days later Dan got the full story of the fate that befell Sam Fletcher. As he staggered his way down the line road with his damaged bicycle, youngsters coming from school looked at the once respectable figure and said, "Hi mister policeman had you an accident with your bike?" His reply was unprintable, the children had no sympathy for him as he had often given them a rough time if he caught them playing ball on the public road. He eventually made his way to the Cross where the line road joined the main road.

Exhausted he sat down on the roadside ditch to rest, there was little motor traffic in those times, but as luck would have it up the road came a transport delivery lorry. Officer Fletcher got to his feet and still in a wobbly state signaled the lorry to stop. The driver, Johnny Cathcart pulled up expecting to be asked for his license and loading documents, for often he had crossed swords with the officious policeman in the past. He was amazed to see the state the officer was in, judging by his appearance he was heavily intoxicated. He pleaded with Johnny to give him and his damaged bicycle a lift back to the station. Between pushing and shoving the lorry driver got the policeman into the passenger's seat of his lorry, put the bike in the back and set off again. He had little sympathy for his passenger for often in the past he given him un-needed annoyance checking his load and documents. Johnny asked him if he had been involved in an accident. Rather incoherently Sam muttered something about returning from a border patrol and in execution of his duties he had collided with a donkey that jumped out of a field in front of him. Soon Johnny turned off the road into the avenue leading to the barracks and parked at the front door. He assisted Sam out of the lorry and led him to the door; he then took the bicycle out of the lorry and placed it against the barrack wall. Lucky there was plenty of room to turn his lorry around without reversing for he wanted to get away as quickly as possible knowing that there would be hell to pay if the Sergeant was in the building. Sam made his way into the day room to report back and fill in a duty sheet on his patrol. The officer on guard duty was shocked and amazed to see the condition his comrade was in. When he realized that Sam was highly intoxicated he was even more shocked. He got Sam away to his room and put him on his bed where he promptly fell asleep. Luckily the Sergeant was in his quarters and did not come on the scene.

Fletcher woke up in the morning with one hell of a hangover knowing that he had to report for duty. He drank several glasses of water not realizing that any person who had imbibed more well than wise of that most potent of all alcoholic beverages – poteen – had only to drink water the next morning which caused a return to the state of the previous evening. Donning his spare uniform he made his way to the duty room where the sergeant was present. He said, "Officer Fletcher, I am aware that you returned to the barrack in a rather sorry looking state yesterday evening. When you have had your breakfast you are to report to my office and make a full report on what happened to you". Sergeant Dundas from years of experience in dealing with intoxicated men understood perfectly that his officer had taken more drink than he could hold. He knew also the after effects of drinking poteen and that by drinking water it could return the person to the state they had been in previously. Fletcher tried to present a case of colliding with the donkey that caused him to have an accident. The sergeant would have none of this, he said, "You are guilty of being in a state of extreme intoxication while on duty, you have caused damage to your uniform which is government property and also left your bicycle unserviceable. You well know that the charges I have put to you merit instant dismissal from the force. I do not know how you got yourself into this unworthy state, not is it my concern how you did so. Nevertheless I am forced to deal with your situation. There are several options that can be taken, I can report you to the District Inspector and you cannot expect any sympathy from him. You will be instantly dismissed. You could tender your resignation from the force and join the army or you can apply for a transfer to Belfast city. Should you take the last option, I will recommend that your application be approved and hopefully this sorry situation you find yourself in can be kept quiet.

I suggest now that you take some days off on sick leave, think over what I have said and report back to me when you are in a fit state to do so". At the end of the week it was a rather subdued and chastened Officer Samuel Fletcher who presented himself at Sergeant Dundas's office and requested a transfer form to move to Belfast. Shortly afterwards the officer with his belongings packed into the standard issue black wooden box and with his now repaired bicycle was transported to the Castle railway station to catch the train to Belfast. There were no regrets at his departure, for an over officious policeman can create problems not only for his comrades but also for relations with the general public. When Dan related the story to Ernst and Paul they were amazed with this subtle manner in which a cute Irishman had dealt with a difficult situation.

Chapter 10

A Body is recovered from the sea

Back at the home base in France the last message had been received from the Junkers plane. There were no reports of a German aircraft having crashed either in Ireland or in England. Colonel Bohmer could only conclude that his most experienced crew and their plane has crashed into the ocean some where off the west coast of Ireland. According to standard procedure the usual messages were sent to the three families notifying them that the crew had been killed in action.

Since the arrival at Dan's farmhouse a little over a week ago so much had happened that the three men were fully occupied at all times. Now when things had settled down there was the danger of boredom setting in and the possibility of them becoming careless. As they sat around the fire after their midday meal Dan said it was time they formed a plan of action to recover the body of their comrade Gerhardt. Ernst realized by now that there was a great bond of friendship between himself, Paul and Dan, and that there was no longer the necessity to remain secretive about the whereabouts of the plane. He explained how their plan to ditch the Junkers into the lake had been successful and that they had made the body of Gerhardt secure in the plane cabin. Dan said that after the explosion and fire on the Croagh he had observed a silent plane glide past his house and come down in Lough Firtry the name of the mountain lake. He complimented Ernst on his skill in bringing the plane down so well and said that the bed of the lake was quite deep in the centre, it was also had soft boggy bottom and the plane would sink into this but not disappear altogether. Because of the nature of the soil the water would never be clear not like some other lakes in the area which had sandy bottoms and on a good clear day a person could see the fish swimming in them. There were no boats on the lakes so there was practically no chance of the plane being discovered.

Ernst said that he and Paul were both good swimmers and could dive well in the water. Dan said that to recover the body would not be terribly difficult, but what then was to be done with it? A secret burial was no solution to the problem, Gerhardt deserved some thing better. Dan recalled how he had read a story in a newspaper about the bodies of four British soldiers being washed ashore on the Sligo coast. They had died when a troop ship had been torpedoed off the west coast of Ireland. Going through a bundle of newspaper cuttings he came across the report on the finding of the bodies and how they had been buried in Ahamish churchyard in County Sligo. The report gave their names and the date of the tragedy, which was on the 7th of August 1940. Dan then made a suggestion, "We can recover Gerhardt's body and secretly transport it to the Atlantic coast, place it in the sea and ensure that it would be discovered. Two purposes would be fulfilled, their comrade would get a proper burial and attention would be diverted from here as it would then be assumed that the Junkers had crashed into the sea with the loss of life of the crew".

Ernst and Paul thought the idea was crazy, but then having witnessed how Dan had planned the down fall of the inquisitive policeman they came to the conclusion that with this crafty farmer anything was possible. Dan said that he had cousins living on the coast at a place called Killdoney and that in his younger days he had spent many days with his relations and often went fishing with them on the sea shore. He said that he regularly supplied his cousins with good quality thatching straw for their cottage and he was soon due to deliver a cart load to them. "Here is my plan. If you men can recover the body from the lake and bring it to the shore we can wrap it securely in a blanket, place it on the cart and build the load of straw over it". He would then set off for the home of his relations and knowing from the days of his visits to the coast that there was a deep pool just on the shore he would place the body into it and arrange for it to be discovered.

It was decided that the search and recovery operation should take place early in the morning before anyone might be about the area. Dan and Sport would keep watch around the lake while Ernst and Paul did the diving. One morning just as dawn was breaking the three men went down to the lake. Conditions were ideal for the exercise. The young Germans had to use some guess work as to the location of the plane. Several dives were made without success, and as it was getting later in the morning the young men decided to have one more try. Within a short time they both came to the surface to say that they had located the plane. As it was now too late to continue they came ashore and placed a marker to indicate were the plane was. All three returned to the house to get warmed up and have a much needed breakfast. They were pleased with progress made so far. It was decided that they should get a long length of rope to attach to the body and take it in to the shore by this means. Dan had two sets of tethers, these being long strong ropes used to secure a large load of hay on a cart. These and a set of reins should be long enough for their purpose.

The following morning conditions were again suitable for a dive, Ernst made the first one and having the rope with him he secured it to Gerhard's body. Paul went down next and freed the body from the position that they had made it secure in. In a short time their mission was accomplished and the body was pulled to the lake shore where Dan was ready with a blanket to wrap it in. Next he brought the cart down from the house and placed the body in it. Dan had made a special frame on the bed of the cart so that when the time was right the body could be removed without disturbing the load of straw. From a drawer in the table Dan produced a rosary that a friend had brought to him while on a pilgrimage to Lourdes in France. This he placed in a pocket of Gerhard's uniform saying, "Now when he is recovered from the sea this will ensure that he will be given a good Christian burial in a Catholic cemetery. With the body safely stowed on the cart the men moved to the farmyard where the large load of straw sheaves was built and securely tied with the tethers. Having had a substantial breakfast Dan departed on his long and sad journey. Ernst and Paul parted company with their good friend and comrade hoping that the plan to have his body discovered would be successful. Dan told them that it would be late evening before he would reach his destination. It was not necessary to warn the men to be vigilant and in any case Sport would carry out his usual guard duties. The route Dan was taking went past Breesy Mountain, through Cashelard, across the main road and then by narrow rural roads to Killdoney. The laneway to the Walsh home stead passed very close to the sea shore. There was a spot there where Dan and his cousin Seamus had fished for salmon. They often managed to catch a good fish in a reasonably deep pool at this place. This was where Dan planned to place Gerhardt's body where it would sink to the bottom and still not be moved by the tide. Getting the cart as close as possible to the pool and making sure that there was nobody around the remote place, he removed the body and placed it into the pool. Before departing to complete his journey Dan with a branch of a tree removed any evidence of the presence of a cart on the shore.

It was now quite dark and in a short time Dan arrived at the home of his cousin where he was made most welcome by Seamus, his wife Connie and their three young children. The first thing he and his cousin did was to remove the sheaves of straw and put then into a shed. Next his horse was attended to before they finally went indoors where a substantial meal had been prepared. Dan of course was as he had expected invited, to stay overnight. When the children of the house had retired to bed, Dan and his cousin Seamus went out side for a smoke and a chat. Dan removed the centre boards from the floor of the cart to reveal the hidden cavity. From it he produced two large packets of tea, several packets of candles, four Cantrell & Cochrane lemonade bottles with screw tops, which contained paraffin oil and a number of packets of white flour and tins of food stuff, all items that were scarce in the Free State. Also in the hidden compartment were two rolled up bicycle tyres and a spare tube. Dan then produced a new bicycle chain and freewheel, all to suit his cousin's bicycle. When all the 'contraband' was brought into the house and stored away they sat down by the fireside for a chat and to catch up on family news. Connie was delighted with all the foodstuff that was nearly impossible to get in the local shops.

As they talked Dan asked Connie how did she come to have that name. She said, "As you know I am a native of County Sligo and we lived near Lissadell the home of the Gore-Booth family. Countess Markievicz that famous Irish woman who took part in the 1916 Rising in Dublin was a member of the Gore-Booth family having been born Constance Gore–Booth. My father, God Rest him was a great admirer of Lady Constance, so when I was born he choose the name for me. Of course in time it became shortened to Connie. As you know I came to work in one of the local hotels and then I met Seamus, so here we are ever since". It was now late and time to retire to bed, for Dan, in the morning had to put the next part of his plan into operation and ensure that the body of Gerhardt was recovered from its place in the sea.

After a good breakfast Dan said he would have set off for home. Seamus had to go into the town on his bicycle and said he would accompany his cousin along the road. Dan was wondering how he would broach the subject of paying a visit to the pool at the sea side without giving a reason for doing so. Then when they were near the place and as luck would have it, a neighbour of Seamus who was a fisherman came running onto the road from the shore in a state of great excitement. John said, "Come quickly to the shore for I have discovered a body in the pool". The three men rushed down and sure enough there was the body of a man in uniform lying in the water. Seamus said that as he had a bicycle he would cycle into the town and notify the Guards. John said that he would remain there until help came. Dan said that as he had a long journey to reach home and that as there was nothing he could do he would be on his way. The others agreed to this and Dan went on his way. It was near evening when he arrived at the house where he was greeted first by Sport and then by Ernst and Paul. He related to the German airman the account of what had taken place and that they could put their minds at ease regarding the recovery of Gerhardt's body.

Several days later Dan got the copy of the local newspaper with the story.

"Local fishermen discover a body in the sea at Killdoney"

The body was removed to the local hospital where an inquest was held. From documents on the body it was identified as that of Gerhardt Distler a member of the German air force. Wounds on the body indicated that the man had died from gunshot wounds. Other injuries were caused by fragments of metal that appeared to be pieces of an aircraft fuselage. This was taken as evidence that his injuries were received when his air craft was shot at by another plane. Contact was made with the German Legation in Dublin who sent a representative to Ballyshannon to make arrangements for the man's funeral. The official informed the police that a German Junkers plane had gone missing while on an exercise from its base in France some days ago. He also confirmed that the airman was one of three men on the crew. He said that it would seem that the plane crashed into the sea somewhere off the west coast of Ireland and that there was a possibility that the bodies of the other two men might also be washed ashore. The official requested that local authorities and fishermen keep a lookout on the shore for further bodies. The discovery of the rosary in the uniform pocket indicated that the man was Catholic; the rosary had come from Lourdes. Following the funeral service in the local Church, the burial took place in the nearby cemetery. Several officials from the German Legation in Dublin attended and full military honours were provided by a contingent of the Irish Army from the nearby Finner Camp.

Dan read the report in the newspaper to his friends, who although sad, were relieved that their comrade had been given a Christian burial and that his family would be informed about this. Now they could concentrate on a plan for Ernst and Paul.

Chapter11

More Escape Plans

Dan understood that naturally his guests were getting restless and bored. The longer they remained in his house the greater the danger of discovery would be. As summer approached there was the likelihood of visitors calling to see Dan. One that he knew was due to call very soon was his nephew Fr. John Bourke who was at present based in Dublin. Due to the outbreak of war Fr. John had to return to Ireland from his post abroad in the Foreign Missions. He knew that he could rely on the priest to keep everything confidential and that it would be safe to introduce him to the two Germans. Ernst and Paul were concerned about their families who would have by now been informed that their plane had crashed at sea and that they were classified as missing in action. Ernst was anxious that by some means he could get a message to Gabriela to let her know that he was still alive. It was unlikely that she would have heard that his plane had gone missing as communication between Germany and Canada would now be non existent.

The next morning Dan got a letter from Fr. John saying that he was arriving by train in Pettigoe on Tuesday 6th May and requesting his uncle to meet him. He planned to stay on the farm for a few days and then return to Dublin before the weekend. In preparation for this Dan took his horse trap out of the shed where it was stored, Ernst or Paul had never seen this type of vehicle and were very intrigued by it. They helped Dan to clean it up, polish the brass fittings, grease the wheel bearings and clean up the decorative wood work on the body of the trap. The special harness also received attention as it was different from the normal horse cart harness. The seat cushions which had been stored in the house were also attended to. The horse was groomed and its shoes checked for missing or loose nails and all was ready in good time to meet the guest.

Early on Tuesday morning Dan set off for Pettigoe to meet the midday train from Dublin. As the train passed through both the Free State and Northern Ireland there were separate carriages for the different passengers. This meant that as Fr. John boarded the train in Dublin and was getting off in Pettigo he did not have to go through a customs check. Ernst and Paul, by now familiar with cooking methods used in a rural farmhouse, had a substantial meal ready for Fr. John and Dan when they arrived back at the house shortly after 2 o'clock. Introductions were made and as Dan had already told the story to the priest of how the German guests had come to be in his home, this was a good topic for discussion during and after the meal. During his career as a priest Fr. John had come across many an unusual experience so he was not really surprised at this story. Of course knowing the type of character his uncle was, nothing about Dan could surprise him. If his uncle could in any way get one over on the authorities he was a happy man. Fr. John was pleased about the plan that had been made to have the body of Gerhardt discovered and that he had been given a Christian burial. He said that he would go to Ballyshannon on one of the days, visit the grave and say a Mass for the young airman. He told the men how he was often called upon to do relief duty for the official Chaplain to the German prisoners of war in the Curragh camp. He knew many of the men in the camp and also had access to the German Legation in Dublin on official duties. He was a fluent speaker in the German language and could converse with the two flyers in their own language. Fr. John was highly amused when he heard about the purchases of clothes made by Dan on the fair day in Belleek. He said that it would be no problem for him to bring Paul back with him to Dublin dressed in a clerical suit and pass him off as a young foreign clerical student. He would have him accommodated in the Mission House in Dublin where he would be safe until a plan was worked out for his immediate future.

Fr. John had a considerable amount of first hand information about the war situation in Europe and he assured the young Germans that in the long term their country would fail in their ambition to control the continent. Knowing that Dan's guests were not members of the Nazi party he advised them that for the duration of the war it would be futile to make any attempt to return to their home land. Once a successful plan for Paul was put into operation, then together they would work some thing out for Ernst. When told about Ernst being anxious to get some form of message to his fiancée – Gabriela in Canada, Fr. John said that even in the Free State all foreign mail was censored; he would give the matter some thought and see what could be done.

The time came for the men to retire for night, Fr. John took over Dan's room and Dan used the 'settle bed' in the kitchen. This piece of furniture was common in Irish farmhouses, during the day it served as a wooden bench to sit on and at night it folded out to form a bed. In the morning over breakfast the discussion on the future of the Germans continued, Fr. John told how already there were nearly 40 German airmen interned in the military prisoner of war camp in the Curragh, Co. Kildare. This was about an hour by bus from Dublin city. The Germans there had survived the crashes of their planes in the south of the country. In the same complex there was also a P.O.W. camp for Allied airmen whose planes had crashed in the Free State. While some of the Germans in the camp were members of the Nazi party, many were not; they had, like Ernst and Paul chosen not to become involved in politics. There was an unusually liberal set of regulations in both camps. The internees were allowed the freedom to go out on parole during the day and they were free to mix with the local people.

They had to return to the camp at night and were honour bound not to escape when out on parole. If they could escape by conventional means from the camp such as building a tunnel or cutting the wire fencing, that was not considered a breach of trust. Even if a German did escape there was no hope of him finding a way back to his home land. One did manage to escape and get aboard a Spanish ship in Dublin port. After leaving Dublin the vessel had to call at an English port; there the escapee was discovered and arrested by the English police and sent to a P.O.W. camp where conditions were not as good as those in Ireland.

Fr. John said that the men could not remain in Dan's house indefinitely; they would eventually be discovered and brought to the Curragh. An enquiry might then lead to the discovery of their hidden aircraft. There was a possible way around the problem for one of the men at this stage, he was aware from his contacts in the camp that there was one prisoner that the German government were most anxious to get back to Germany. He was Rudolf Ludwig, a highly qualified aeronautical engineer who had been testing new equipment on a plane when it was attacked by British fighters and then force landed in neutral Ireland. The aircraft was set on fire after it had crashed and the secret equipment destroyed. If this man left the camp and got refuge in the German Legation in Dublin his absence would be immediately discovered by the Irish authorities. There was a way to overcome the problem and it depended very much on Paul being willing to play an important part in the plan. He would accompany Fr. John to Dublin and move into the Mission house. The technician would come to Dublin city while out on parole and visit the house. There the men would exchange their positions with Paul taking the name of Rudolf Ludwig whose name would be on the parole pass. He would become part of a group of Germans returning to the camp in the place of his countryman. There would be nobody missing when a check was made on the number of prisoners and no alarm would be raised. It would then be up to the staff in the Legation to get the real Rudolf aboard a neutral ship which would take him to its home country and safety. It was a daring plan, which would have a good chance to succeed as there would be nobody reported as missing. Paul said he was agreeable to play his part in the plan for as things stood he would eventually end up in the Curragh anyhow. Fr. John said that if this was successful they would work something out for Ernst; in any case one person in Dan's house could be explained in some way. Ernst with his first class command of the English language could be passed off as a nephew of Dan's.

Later in the morning Dan and Fr. John set of in the horse and trap for Ballyshannon where the priest visited the grave of Gerhardt. Having some friends who were Nuns in the local convent he arranged to say a private Mass in the convent chapel for Gerhardt. After the Mass both men were treated to a substantial meal by the good sisters who seemed to never suffer from the rationing of foodstuffs. Before leaving for home again Fr. John made a few purchases in a local shop. The significance of one item would be of great benefit to Ernst. The only caller to come near the house was the postman, who on finding the door locked would leave any letters in one of the out houses. Paul and Ernst were in the house, Sport was on guard outside. They took the opportunity to lift the stone flag from the kitchen floor and removed Paul's uniform and documents from the hiding place and replaced the stone again. The uniform was brushed clean, ironed and dried in front of a good turf fire; it was going to be necessary for Paul to have his uniform in the P.O.W. camp if the plan succeeded. Dan had left Paul out a small suitcase to carry his belongings in.

Late in the evening Fr. John and Dan arrived home to be greeted by Sport and the two young men. After their evening meal the men sat around the fire to talk and relax, it was then that Fr. John produced one of his purchases from his pocket. It was a simple postcard with an Irish scene pictured on it. He instructed Ernst to write a brief message on it, address it to Gabriela in Canada and he would post it from Dublin. All mail was strictly censored but nobody would expect any hidden details on a simple postcard. Ernst wrote a short message: -

Dear Gabriela, You will be pleased to learn that I am thankfully recovering from my recent accident. I suffered no serious injuries, just got a little bit shook up. I am spending some time here in Dublin with my uncle and I really miss taking Rex for his daily walk. I trust you keep well and I will soon write you a letter.

Slainte – E.S.

The card was addressed to Miss Gabi O'Reilly in Canada. Fr. John would post the card in Dublin along with the mail from his religious house so that it would have a good chance to not attract any attention.

The next morning, Thursday 8th May, the men were up early; Paul was dressed up in his clerical suit and did look very impressive, especially when he donned his black hat. To hide the fact that he did not have a clergyman's collar he wore a fine white scarf around his neck. His uniform was placed in the suitcase of Fr. John and covered in clerical vestments. With the horse harnessed into the trap, they were ready to set off to catch the train to Dublin in Pettigoe. The parting of the two German friends was naturally emotional; by some means they would keep in contact. As they were about to depart Fr. John asked Ernst if he had a photograph of himself in civilian clothing saying that he was considering another plan for him. Ernst did have a picture of himself and Gabriela taken before she left for Canada, this he gave to the priest. Fr. John promised to return to Donegal within a short time when he had thought of some thing for Ernst. At the station the priest gave his return ticket to Paul and purchased a single for himself. They bid farewell to Dan and in a short time were seated in the Dublin carriage on the train. This carriage would not be subject to any checks by customs or police as the train made its way through Fermanagh to re-enter the Free State at Clones.

The two men arrived safe in Dublin and were made welcome in the Mission House in Dublin. The members there asked no questions about the new guest for they were well used to the clandestine activities of Fr. John. Paul was shown to a room where he dispensed with his clerical garb and dressed in his civilian clothes. The following day Fr. John took Paul out for walks in the city so that he could become familiar with Dublin. Being in the company of a priest, meant that he did not attract any undue attention. It all felt so strange to him but he soon learned to relax and enjoy it all. On Sunday, Fr. Bourke was scheduled to attend the German P.O.W. camp in the Curragh to carry out the duties of Chaplain.

After the service in the camp was over and Fr. John had attended to the spiritual needs of the German Catholics he asked for a meeting with Ober Leutenant Kurt Mullenhaser, one of the senior German officers. In privacy he put the proposed plan for the freedom of

Rudolf and his possible return to Germany. The Leutenant was very enthusiastic about the proposal and agreed that it was well worth attempting. He would go into the city in the morning and as he was entitled to do, pay a call to the German Legation and put the proposal to Dr. Hemshall. Fr. John returned to Dublin feeling content that the plan would be a success. He had arranged to meet with the Ober Leutenant on Monday afternoon in one of the hotels and get a report on the views of Dr. Hemshall. Kurt told Fr. John that the Doctor was all for the idea and that it should be put into operation without delay as a ship would be leaving for another neutral country before the end of the week and he could arrange to have Rudolf Ludwig smuggled on board. The Ober Leutenant said that on Thursday the 15th of May a group of the prisoners would apply for parole and come to Dublin for the day. Rudolf would be one of the party. Fr. Bourke and Paul would meet the group in a city hotel in the afternoon.

This went ahead as planned and Fr. John accompanied by Paul, who was dressed in civilian clothes, brought his uniform with him in a small suitcase. Paul and Rudolf were introduced to each other and with several members of the group they went to the cloak room of the hotel where their comrades kept watch while Paul changed into his uniform and Rudolf dressed in the civilian garments, which were a reasonable fit for him. Rudolf also gave Paul his pass which was necessary to get into the camp. Rudolf was then met by a member of staff from the Legation who took him away to a safe house from where he would be taken aboard the ship. Fr. John parted company with the Germans and told Paul that he would see him on his next visit to the camp.

In the evening the German prisoners returned by bus to the Curragh. There they presented their passes to the guard on duty who had no idea that a switch in persons had been carried out. Paul got a great welcome from his countrymen but on the advice of the Ober Leutenant gave no information on the fate of his plane nor did he say anything about his comrade Ernst Schmitt. In a few days word came to Kurt that the operation had been fully successful and that Rudolf would soon be safe in a neutral country and on his way home to Germany. Naturally the story of the only German prisoner to successfully escape from Ireland during World War 2 had to be kept a close secret.

Chapter 12

Ernst Schmitt gets a new identity

Back on the farm near the border everything was a lot quieter, Dan encouraged Ernst to move out and about so that made life easier for both of them. There was the occasional caller to visit Dan. If he knew them and trusted them he introduced 'Ernie' as he called him, as a nephew who had suffered injuries when the English city he lived in was bombed. He was staying with Dan until he was fully recovered. For other callers to the farm Ernst took refuge in the secret apartment. On Thursday 22nd May a letter arrived from Fr. John to say that Paul had now settled into his new position and he was happy there and got on well with his comrades at work. Fr. John said he would be back again for a short visit to Donegal at the end of the month. In the house and about the farm Dan and Ernst held many conversations. Dan explained the purpose of the talks. He wanted Ernst to develop as far as possible a local accent and use words that were in everyday use. This was not a big problem for Ernst as when he and Gabriela had practiced talking in the English language during their student days he had learned a lot from her.

The two men kept busy on the farm, Ernst was a good worker who could adapt too many tasks. The single horse mowing machine was in need of a good overhaul so he told Dan what parts were required and he fitted them. He also dismantled, cleaned and replaced the worn parts in the Vermoral Éclair knapsack potato spraying machine. The men spent several days in the bog cutting turf, a new experience for Ernst and something he took a great interest in. On Monday 1st June Dan harnessed up the horse and trap to go to Pettigoe railway station to collect Fr. John Bourke. This time he brought Ernst with him. This was quite an experience for Ernst to see some of the Irish countryside that he had only observed from the air. For a change the three men had their midday meal in the local hotel. Several of the locals came to greet Dan and Fr. John. They accepted without question Ernst as a friend of the family, but generally the conversation centered on the older men. On the way home the priest brought them up to date on Paul and how he had been accepted into life in the P.O.W. camp. He also told them that Rudolf had made it safely back to Germany. There he was quietly able to get word to Ernst's parents to let them know that their son was safe and well in Ireland.

When they returned to the house and had got settled down around the fire, Fr. John explained to Ernst why he had required his photograph. Having done some research he had found a new identity for Ernst and he was now in a position to get him a legal Irish passport. A search through one of the big city cemeteries had produced the name of a Michael E. Smith who had died in infancy over twenty years ago. With this information Fr. John was able to get a birth certificate and the other necessary documents to procure a passport. He had with him an application form to apply for this, all that was required was for Ernst to fill in the form and sign it. As a priest he was qualified to vouch for Ernst, with this being done he would bring all the documents to the appropriate government department. He was already well known to the officials there and should have no problem in getting the passport. He had become well known in the office when applying for passports and travel documents for religious persons going abroad to work on the missions. "I have a plan in mind for you Ernst when I have this stage completed. There will be an element of danger involved and I am sure you are prepared to take any necessary risks to give you a decent future in life. When I return here in a short time I will have every thing organized for you".

When all the paper work had been completed; the three men retired to bed for the night. In the morning Fr. John said that if Dan would drive him to Ballyshannon he would visit Gerhardt's grave and again say a Mass for him in the Convent Chapel. This time they would take Ernst with them so he could pay his respects to his dead comrade. Fr. John would then take the train from there to Dublin. John and Ernst would travel by road to the house. On his return to the city the priest went to the passport office and left the documents for processing with an official he knew. It would be ready in two weeks time. His next call was to the office of the Irish Shipping Company at the Dublin docks. He made enquiries about another friend of his who was Captain of one of the merchant ships. This company was set up by the Irish Government in March 1941 so that the country could import and export essential goods during the war. Britain had decided that it could no longer put its ships and men at risk by supplying a country that had decided to remain neutral. A Greek ship that had been abandoned in Spain was purchased by the Irish Government. A Captain J. Moran and an Irish crew set sail for Dublin with a full cargo of grain. This first ship in the fleet was re-named 'The Irish Popular'.

In due course a respectable merchant fleet was built up by the Irish authorities. Goods were imported from Spain, Africa, the United States of America and Canada. The Irish vessels were permitted to join in the allied convoys up through the Bay of Biscay and on the North Atlantic route. Although the ship flew the flag of a neutral country and had the words - EIRE – painted in large letters on their sides and on the deck they were not immune from attack by German U-Boats and aircraft. At least 16 Irish merchant ships were lost during World War 2. Some hit mines, others were bombed by aircraft and many more torpedoed by U-boats. At least 150 Irish seamen perished along with their ships. When a convoy was attacked by U-boats and ships sunk; the other ships were under strict orders not to stop and pick up survivors from the sea as such action would further endanger the convoy. The Captains of several Irish ships chose to ignore these instructions and would always stop and carry out a rescue with the result that the lives of over 500 Allied seamen were saved by Irish merchant ships.

When the Irish Shipping Company was formed it was extremely difficult for the Government to find any other country willing to sell or lease to them ships. A senior Government Minister was sent to America in an endeavour to purchase ships. Sad to say, undue influence was brought to bear on the authorities in Washington not to accommodate the Irish. The unspoken reason being, that the stance of neutrality taken in Ireland did not warrant them being given any ships. Ireland was not without friends in high places. The minister was directed to a very high ranking lady officer of Irish ancestry in the U.S. Navy who was sympathetic towards the land of her fore-bearers. The result was that the minister got his ships. Captain Brian O'Connor a personnel friend of Fr. John Bourke was the master of 'The Irish Sycamore' one of the former American ships that had been purchased and re-named. The Manager of the company informed Fr. John that 'The Irish Sycamore' was due into the home port within a week with a cargo of supplies from Canada. She would take at least another week to unload, get re-fueled and any necessary servicing carried out before sailing in convoy again for Halifax in Canada. During that period Fr. John could arrange to meet with his friend Captain O'Connor.

Chapter 13

A Pilot sails to Canada

A few days after 'The Irish Sycamore' had docked in Dublin Fr. John paid a visit to his old friend Captain Brian O'Connor on the 6th June. The Captain had a great welcome for the priest and leaving the ship they went to a nearby restaurant for a meal. There was much general talk about the days of their youth and then of course on the situation now with the war and all the problems that it had brought. Brian told all about the dangers of his voyages in the convoys and the dangers from the U-boats. Then Fr. John said, "Brian, I have a problem that I need you help with, if you are willing to give it to me". The Captain said, "Knowing you Fr. John and having experience of the things you can get up to I had guessed that you did have something up your sleeve. Let me hear what you have to say".

Fr. John then made his request known "I have a very good and reliable friend who needs to get from Ireland to Canada where his fiancée now resides with her Aunt. He is not a criminal, nor is he wanted by the authorities in connection with any political or other offence. His record is perfectly clean; he has a valid passport and all the necessary documents to travel abroad. He has excellent mechanical engineering qualifications and would be an ideal assistant in the engine room of your vessel. I would be extremely grateful if you could see it your way to sign him on as a member of your crew for your next voyage to Canada. I will not expect you to give me a decision right away, but at least think it over and come back to me in a few days". The priest said that there was some thing more to his request that was confidential between him and his friend but on another occasion he would tell Brian the full story.

The two friends met again over a meal on the afternoon of Monday 8th June. Captain Brian said, "I have given a lot of thought to your proposal and if you can assure me that everything is straight and above board I will take the chance and sign up your friend as an engine room assistant. As I am sure you are aware this is one of the most dangerous position on any ship, for in the event of an attack by U-boats or aircraft there is no hope of escape from the engine room. Under war conditions I do have great difficulty in getting dependable men for the trans-Atlantic voyages. Therefore the authorities do not question my right to chose crew members. I take it that your friend will leave the ship in Halifax if we do manage to get there. This will leave me shorthanded for the return trip, but I may manage to find a replacement during the time I will be in Halifax. It will take me at least two weeks to unload my ship and take on the cargo for Ireland. Then it takes several more days to find a place in a westward bound convoy. I will expect your friend to remain with me until just before I sail for home as I need the help of all hands when in harbour in Canada. I will pay him the standard wage in Canadian currency as this is what he will need in that country". Fr. John thanked his friend for his help and said, "As you plan to depart from Dublin by Saturday the 13th June I will have my friend here with you a few days before hand". The following morning the priest collected the passport from the office and caught the train for Pettigoe. Not having time to send a letter, he sent a telegram to Dan asking him to meet the Dublin train at the station Wednesday 10th June.

Dan and Ernst now realized that the time was fast approaching when they would have to part company. One evening they took a walk down by the shore of the lake and Ernst pointed out to Dan where his Junkers aero-plane now rested. He showed him where he and Paul had hidden the inflatable dinghy and told him when everything had settled down that he should recover it and maybe find a use for it on the lake. A very strong bond of friendship had developed between the men and Dan was going to miss having the company around the house. Whatever Fr. John had in store for Ernst, the friends would find some way to keep in contact. Having received the telegram, the men duly collected Fr. John at the station. On their way home he told them of the plans he had made to get Ernst to Canada on the ship captained by his friend. The voyage would not be without risks for there was always the danger of being torpedoed by a U-boat. If all was a success Ernst would be reunited with Gabriela and the O'Reilly family in Toronto.

As they talked over a meal, Fr. John told Ernst that he would be acting as an assistant to the Chief Engineer in the engine department on the ship. His college training and experience with his father in the workshop would ensure that he would be more than useful anywhere that there were engines. Ernst wondered how it would be safe to get a message to Gabriela without giving the censors cause to be suspicious. Fr. John explained that he had arranged with Captain O'Connor that Ernst should join the ship immediately at the Dublin docks. On arrival in Halifax the ship would be at least two or three weeks there to unload and take on board the cargo for Ireland.

He suggested that Ernst should have a letter written and ready to post as soon as the ship docked. A letter would arrive in Toronto within a few days and being an internal letter would not be subject to censorship. This would give Gabriela time to get some days off work and travel eastwards by train to Halifax. He also said that she should bring the O'Reilly children with her so that when the group would return by train to Toronto they would not attract the attention that Ernst would if traveling alone. Before finally mailing the letter Ernst should find a hotel where he could get accommodation and where he could meet with the family. The priest said that Captain O'Connor would pay Ernst the standard wage for a seaman and that he would be paid in Canadian dollars.

In the dresser in Dan's kitchen, as there was in all Irish farm houses was a set of big crockery mugs with matching bowls. Going to one of them Dan took it down to the table, lifted off the bowl and from the mug he removed a bundle of notes. Turning to Ernst he said, "My sister in Canada regularly sends me money that I do not always have a use for. You are to take it and it means that you will be financially independent until you get a job in Canada, some thing I am sure the husband of Gabriela's aunt will arrange for you". Ernst was shocked at this and said, "Dan you and Fr. John have already done so much for me and not without considerable risk to both of you. I cannot possibly encroach on your generosity any further". Dan said it is absolutely necessary that you should have Canadian currency when you get there. Just take the money as a loan that you can repay it when you have found employment. This war will not last for ever and when peace comes you can come here and enjoy a proper holiday. Fr. John gave his full support to Dan leaving Ernst little choice but to agree to the plan. The flying uniform was to remain in its secure hiding place with the priest now aware of its existence.

In the morning of Thursday 11th June, with the meager belongings of Ernst packed in a small case provided by Dan the men set off for the station at Pettigoe. As he left the house that had been his home for many weeks Ernst had a long look down to the lake where his plane remained hidden. Sport, his canine friend lay on the street at the door of the house with his head sunk between his paws. He knew something out of the ordinary was going on. As Ernst put his hand down to pat the dog, Sport licked the hand with a sad look in his eyes. This was his farewell. At the station Dan gave his German friend a piece of paper with the address of his sister in Canada on it and made him promise to look her up. The final parting was silent and solemn; but as men are wont to do, they kept their emotions hidden. For both Dan and Ernst their lives would never again be the same again.

Chapter 14

A Final Voyage

Fr. John and Ernst found a compartment in the Dublin carriage which had no other passengers; therefore they could talk in private. Ernst told the priest all about his father's service in the First World War and how he had correctly judged the dangers of the Nazi regime. He told him how his fiancée had come to be in Canada at this particular time, where she lived with the Irish husband of her aunt Margret. Due to his several years of service abroad the priest was in a position to advise Ernst on many simple things that could indicate his real nationality. The spelling of his name should now become Ernest or for short Ernie, Schmitt would become Smith, a very common name in Ireland and England. He would have to be careful in the use of recording numerals, for example the 1 & 7 had a distinctive way of being written in Germany compared to the English/Irish and American way.

When working with comrades on the ship or elsewhere, the men he would be working with, particularly Irishmen, had a subtle means of finding out all about you, where you were born, where you lived and all about your family. "As you know the name on your passport is that of a young man who died at an early age many years ago. There are no known relations of his still alive in Ireland. What you will do is prepare your own story. You are the son of a single mother and you were born in a home where these unfortunate young women were taken and kept until the birth of their baby. The girls were, to say the least not treated kindly by the staff in the homes and soon after their baby was born it was taken away from its mother for adoption. In your case you were adopted by an Irish couple who lived in the city of Manchester in England. You had a real good home there and your adopted parents treated you like a natural son".

"When Manchester was bombed by the Germans in 1940 your home was destroyed and you were injured. Your parents escaped unharmed but because they were so concerned for your safety your mother decided to send you over to Ireland to live with her brother Dan in Donegal. Because of your injuries you would have been exempt from conscription into the forces on medical grounds. You still wanted to do your bit during the war and so you chose to join the merchant navy. The dangers aboard a merchant ship were much greater than that which would be experienced in the regular forces. Your story will be fully acceptable to the men you will work along with on board The Irish Sycamore. You will not be seen as shirking your duties towards your country in a time of war. Your training in the engineering department in a technical college gives you the necessary qualifications to be an assistant in the engine room of the ship". Ernst asked Fr. John would he if possible, through his acquaintances in the German Legation, get word to his parents and Gabriela's mother that he was alive and well. They in turn would find a means of getting a message to Colonel Karl Bohmer with the information.

On arrival in Dublin the men took a bus out to the Mission House where Ernest stayed for the night. In the morning Fr. John made arrangements to bring his friend to the quays and introduced him to Captain O' Connor. The Captain in turn introduced him to the Chief Engineer – Bob Flaherty – who would be addressed as 'Chief'. From then on there would be little or no contact between Ernest and the Captain. He went back on deck and took his leave from his great friend Fr. John Bourke.

Meanwhile in Germany and in the town of Pulheim, Dieter was kept very busy in his workshop. So great was the demand for aircraft parts that he had to employ extra staff. He and Elsa decided that it would be advisable for Susanna to leave her apartment and move into a room in their home. Because Susanna's late husband had been Jewish they felt that she might be in some danger from the authorities. Dieter also gave her a job in the factory office where all orders were taken and processed. This ensured that Susanna was doing important work for the government and so would not attract any suspicion. One day in June a dreaded message came to Dieter and Elsa to tell them that their son Leutenant Ernst Schmitt had been lost in action when his plane crashed at sea. Deepest sympathy was offered to the family on their sad loss. Naturally the family was devastated on receiving this sad news. Along with Susanna they realized that under the circumstances of the time there was no means of getting this news to Gabriela in Canada. Then one morning in July a military motor car arrived at the house, a passenger in the uniform of a high ranking officer came to the door and asked to speak to Dieter and Elsa in privacy. They invited him in and he introduced himself as Colonel Karl Bohmer and that he had been their son's commanding officer in the Luftwaffe. It being a pleasant day the Colonel suggested that they take the coffee that Elsa had prepared in the garden. When seated around the table he said, "Prepare yourselves for some news on your son. You will have remarked that I did not offer you my sympathy on your loss. I am happy to inform you that your son is alive and well on the island of Ireland. With one of his crew he survived the crash of his plane into the Atlantic Ocean. This information, you must understand is to be treated with the utmost secrecy, even my senior officers are not aware of the situation. It was passed to me in a way that must remain confidential. Some day you will learn the full story. You must continue to express an outward show of grief to your neighbours and friends. The official reason for my visit to you today is to give you my condolences to you as a comrade and friend of your son". With that the Colonel took his leave of the grateful parents.

In the engine room of the Irish Sycamore, Chief Flaherty showed Ernest where his bunk was. There he left his belongings. The Chief said, "I do not know what engineering qualifications you have, but I am committed to giving you a job. There is much work to be done here before we sail on Saturday. I want you to make sure that this room is kept clean and tidy at all times. You are to check the fuel tanks and be sure that there are no signs of any leaks. Check the lubrication storage tanks in the same way". Ernest replied, "I have studied mechanical engineering at college, I can operate a lathe, do both acetylene and electric welding and carry out many other tasks that you may find useful". Ernest was supplied with overalls and other protective clothing necessary for his work. He made himself familiar with the lay out of the engine room, checked all the tools and equipment much of which was similar to that which he had used in his fathers workshop and in the college in Köln. He cleaned and made tidy all the tools on the work benches, checked the welding cylinders for gas, did a check on the lathe and other equipment. Unknown to him the Chief had observed all of this and concluded that this new crew man could with some training become a valued member of his staff.

During the next few days the ship was a hive of activity as cargo for Canada was taken aboard and stored in the hold. Ernest was introduced to other members of the engine room staff and found them good company and easy to get along with. They accepted him into their group and as he had been forewarned by Fr. John, many questions were asked of him about his background and his family. The men themselves were quite familiar with the social conditions prevailing in Ireland at the time and could relate to the conditions that Ernest was reared in. It was late on the evening of Saturday 13th June when the Irish Sycamore cast off from the Dublin docks and set sail northwards up the Irish Sea into the North Channel, where off the coast from Belfast a convoy of some eighty vessels was being assembled for the voyage across the Atlantic Ocean to Canada.

It was while waiting to get all the ships into position that Ernest while cleaning the engine components; discovered a fracture in the mounting plate of a lubrication oil circulating pump. He pointed this out to his immediate superior who then brought it to the attention of the Chief. Ernest said that if the plate was removed it could be welded and left fully serviceable. The Chief gave the go ahead for the work to be carried out; he realized that there was time to do the job before the convoy departed. He also knew that if the plate had broken at sea the engines would have had to be stopped until the repair was done and the ship would have lost its place in the convoy. A team of the engine room staff put a temporary support under the oil pump and removed the damaged plate, Ernest cut a deep grove along the fracture, made the plate secure in a jig and proceeded to weld the fracture. When this was complete he asked the Chief to inspect the repair. He was delighted with the workmanship on the plate and gave permission to have it replaced under the oil pump. Later when the job was complete the Chief came to Ernest, complimented him first on detecting the fault and praised the other crew members who had helped carry out the repairs.

It was to be Saturday 20th of June before the convoy was full assembled and set off around the north coast of Donegal on its way to Canada protected by British war ships. When not on watch duties Ernest was permitted to go on deck to get some fresh air and observe the other ships regularly change direction in a zig - zag pattern so as not to make a good target for attacking U- boats. All the time the protecting battle ships kept guard on the ships. Some distance out from the west coast of Ireland the convoy was joined by flying boat's, Ernest knew that the Sunderland's and Catalina's were from Lough Erne as he had often seen them pass over the farm of his friend Dan Mooney. The Irish Sycamore had been allocated a position at the end of the convoy; important ships such as tankers passenger carrying vessels and others occupied places in the centre of the convoy where they were less in danger of being torpedoed.

The convoy was about mid-way across the Atlantic, when early on the morning of Thursday 25th June the alarm was raised that a U-boat was in the area. A torpedo was fired at a small merchant vessel at the rear of the convoy and scored a hit. Many of the crew jumped over board. Some had life jackets and others clung to pieces of wreckage. Captain O'Connor immediately ordered his ship to turn around and go to the rescue of the stricken sailors. He managed to get 15 men aboard the Irish Sycamore before rejoining the convoy. Allied ships in convoys were under strict orders not to leave the group and pick up survivors as by doing so they could endanger the other ships. Irish vessels belonging to a neutral country were not bound by these orders. The rest of the voyage was uneventful and on Tuesday 30th June the convoy reached the safety of the port of Halifax in Nova Scotia.

Chapter 15

Toronto at Last

With the Irish vessel securely in the dock in Halifax city, preparations were made for the unloading of its cargo. It would be here for at least three weeks before the essential supplies for Ireland were taken aboard. On Wednesday 1st July Ernest applied for and was granted shore leave. He had asked the opinion of some of his more experienced ship mates about seeking hotel accommodation in the city. He was told that due to a strong Irish influence in Nova Scotia that it would not be a problem booking a room and an assistant manageress in a large Nova Scotia Hotel would be most helpful to anyone from Ireland. Ernest went to the hotel and asked for the lady by name, giving the name of his comrade who had recommended him to her. He said that he had just arrived from Ireland and was a crew member of the Irish Sycamore; he had relations in Toronto who had invited him to visit them during his stay in Canada. As he had not been able to give them any idea of when he would be in Halifax he would write to them and they would travel to the east coast by train and spend some time with him.

The manageress said that this could be arranged and Ernest used the Canadian dollars given to him by Dan to pay a deposit on the accommodation. He presented his passport and other documents for identification purposes, then completed the letter to Gabriela telling her of his arrival in Halifax and inviting her to travel eastwards by train to meet him there. The train station was in North Street, adjacent to the hotel. She was if possible to bring with her Eva and Michael her cousins and Ernest could return with them to Toronto. He immediately sent the letter of by post. Back on board the ship he asked to meet with Captain O'Connor to acquaint him of his plans for the future and that all being well he would join his fiancée in Toronto. Ernest said that he would stay with the ship and do any necessary work in preparation for the return voyage. The Captain said he would be sorry to loose this valuable crew member but that he understood the position Ernest was in. He then gave the young man his wages for the voyage plus a generous bonus for the good work that he had done. Ernest told the Captain that when he returned to Dublin his friend Fr. John Bourke would give him the full story of how it was necessary that he should get to Canada.

Within a week he had a letter from Gabriela expressing surprise and joy that he was now in Canada. She would travel by train with her cousins and arrive in Halifax on the evening of Friday 10th July. In the afternoon of that day Ernest bade farewell to his comrades, to Chief Engineer Flaherty and to Captain Brian O'Connor. It was a most joyful reunion when Ernest greeted Gabriela and her cousins when they stepped off the train at the station. The group checked into the hotel and over a meal there was so much news to be exchanged. The next morning Gabriela, Ernest, Eva and Michael boarded the west bound train for Toronto to be reunited with the O'Reilly family.

Chapter 16

A letter to Dan.

Toronto,

Canada, 3rd September 1941.

Dear Dan,

Now that I have reached the safety of this fine country I can let you know all about my safe arrival here in this wonderful city. Gabriela and her two cousins traveled to meet me in Halifax and brought me back to the O'Reilly family home. There I was made so welcome and treated as one of the family. Peter has even managed to find me employment in an engineering works in the city.

I cannot even begin to thank you for all you have done for me and for my comrades. Give my best wishes and thanks to Fr. John for his wonderful help. Some day this dreadful war will be over; then I will bring Gabriela, who will then be my wife, to Ireland to meet you in person. Do write and let me know how you are keeping. I have made contact with your sister and will be meeting her and the family within a few weeks.

Kindest regards from your friend,

Ernest Smith.

About the Author

For some years Joe O'Loughlin contributed stories of local interest to local newspapers, principally the Belleek page of the Fermanagh News, edited by Willie John Duffy.

He is a member of The Clogher Historical Society, The Donegal Historical Society. The Churchill and Tully Castle Historical Society and the Friends of the County Fermanagh Castle Museum. He has been regularly interviewed on radio and television on matters pertaining to the World War 11 period in Fermanagh and the Flying Boats on Lough Erne. He has worked along with the Irvinestown historian and broadcaster, Breege McCusker in having memorial stones erected on many of the air craft crash sites associated with Lough Erne and the Donegal Corridor. He has also contributed articles to The Clogher Historical society journal and reviewed articles by other authors for the journal. Some of his books have been reviewed in the Clogher and Donegal journals. He has assisted students with information where they had chosen the World War 11 period as the subject for their history examinations. He has advised and guided new authors in how to have their work published and has proof read many works for other authors.

He is always willing to give talks to Historical Society groups, schools libraries and museums.

Dedication

This is for me book number seven, not many years ago I would never have foreseen that I might some day become an author. It is but right that this book should be dedicated to a number of people who have helped me over the years. First must be my wife Ina who has always supported this hobby of mine, then our sons and daughters, my brothers and sisters who have always had an interest in the books I had published. I can say that I served a rather amateurish apprenticeship to journalism under the guidance of Willie John Duffy, editor of the Belleek page in the Fermanagh news. Willie would often ask me to contribute a report on matters of local interest. He would correct my many errors and add his own sense of humour to what otherwise would be a basic story.

Book number one, the first real attempt to produce a proper book was, when in 1992 Ann Monaghan, Charlie Ward and myself compiled, "The Church Upon the Hill" to mark the centenary of St. Patrick's Church, Belleek. Two good friends who contributed to this book are sadly no longer with us, Sister Elizabeth Smith wrote a moving letter of how she grew up in the parish. Fr. Seamus McManus then Parish Priest of Aghaloo, Aughnacloy wrote the Preface. The art work of our daughter Jane illustrated incidents of the pre camera age in a way that contributed immensely to the enjoyment of the readers.

Book number two a history of the "West Fermanagh Kingdoms of Mulleek and Toura" was produced in 1998 under the guidance of noted Irvinestown historian, author and highly valued friend, Breege McCusker who also kindly wrote the foreword. The graphic design and layout was done expertly by James McGrath then on the staff of the Donegal Democrat. The Preface was written by another family friend of long standing, Rev. Nigel D.J. Kirkpatrick, B.Th. of St. Columba's Church, Portadown. Once again the art work of daughter Jane has by her illustrations added in no small way to the production of this book.

Book number three, was in 2003 the first venture into the realm of fiction. "The Phantom Airman" is a mixture of fiction and historical fact covering 1500 years. This story owes its existence to journalist - Gerry McLaughlin – who in the Irish News, Sept. 19th 1992 wrote an article containing memories of World War 11 in the Belleek district. He suggested that an airman based in one of the radio stations in Belleek had imbibed more well that wise in a rural Shebeen had lost his way while crossing the bog on a foggy night and was never seen again. Gerry wrote that there was the making of a great story slumbering somewhere in Fermanagh on this mythical person. Being then busy working on 'The Church Upon the Hill' I preserved the article in place where things to be done are stored. I felt that the story was so good that it would need the talents of a professional writer. I suggest this to a number of such people who for one reason or another did not consider it suitable. The best advice I got was when I discussed it with Mary Pat Kelly, New York T.V. producer and journalist who said to me, "Joe if you want that book written, just do it your self". Having prepared the manuscript I invited a number of well qualified friends to read it and proof read it and give me their opinion on the merits of the story. Breege McCusker was most enthusiastic, Susan Catherine Schneider, author of Oregon, U.S.A., Maire Carr, a legal secretary, London, my sister Eileen Aiken, retired teacher, Ardee, Co. Louth, Anne Palmer, journalist, Enniskillen, her aunt Kathleen Palmer, Librarian, Enniskillen, my nephew, Brian O'Loughlin, newspaper editor, Jutta Tyler, Author, Kinlough, Co. Leitrim. Patricia Brooks, author and retired school teacher of New Zealand whose ancestors came from Belleek. Having read and corrected my many mistakes all of the above keep the pressure on me to have "The Phantom Airman" published. Soon the manuscript was presented to James McGrath and his worthy assistant, my cousin Sinead Fox. James was by now managing Diamond Sign Printing, again he did an excellent design on this book.

Book number four "Voices of the Donegal Corridor" contains many stories of the planes that crashed in Fermanagh and Donegal during World War 11 was published by Nonsuch, Dublin in 2005. Once again Breege McCusker made a major contribution to this book as did the families of airmen from various parts of the world. They supplied me with very valuable information and useful photographs. For the many ceremonies we held to unveil memorial stones in memory of the young airmen who died in crashes we received invaluable help from Commandant Sean Curran of the 28th Infantry Battalion, Finner Camp, Ballyshannon. This book was launched for me in the Fermanagh County Library, Enniskillen by Edward O'Loghlin of the Medical Library, Galway University. Edward was the organiser of the 2005 O'Loughlin Clan Reunion in The Burren, Co. Clare.

Book number five "Old Belleek Town" also published by Nonsuch in 2006. For this I received many previously unpublished photographs from a number of local people who wish to remain nameless. It has also been enhanced by the art work of Jane O'Loughlin. It brought great pleasure to the many exiles from the area now living in far off countries.

Book number six "A History of Camlin Castle and the Tredennick Family". Here I revert once again to self publishing and avail of the expertise of James McGrath and Diamond Sign Printing. The finished product is proof of this decision. My thanks once again to Breege McCusker for her support and fitting Foreword. I was fortunate that Camlin Castle was perhaps the only major building and family estate in the area that had not already been historically documented. The arrival in Belleek in September 2006 of Wendy Tredennick/Henderson and her cousin Mary Tredennick who sought my help in tracing the family connection to the area provided me with the incentive and invaluable information to proceed with this work. Wendy kindly wrote a most suitable Preface for the book. At a later stage their cousin Jenny who lives in Magherafelt joined the team.

The tragic death of local journalist Donna Marie Ferguson in whose memory the book is dedicated is suitably coupled with the history of Camlin Castle. In the planning and design of the book I was ably guided and advised by another good friend – Eileen Hewson – a highly talented author in a different field.

Book number seven is a return to the realm of fiction. A rumour circulated in this area during World War 11 that a German plane had crashed into the moor lands and disappeared without trace led me to write a story 'Lost in Ireland'. Once again I have been advised and guided by Eileen Hewson and of course my usual adviser – Breege McCusker. With so many faithful advisors and friends it is not a wonder that my publications have been successful considering my status as an amateur who lacks any academic qualifications. To all these wonderful people I dedicate this work.